"W

"What do you think we ... a subdued voice.

"Stay with me. Can you swim?"

"Will we have to?"

"I don't know."

The horses were screaming in a panic Slocum recognized as desperation. He rose and opened the door to see outside. Water lapped at the floor of the coach. There wouldn't be much time to make a good decision. They were stopped in a choppy sea of fast-rising water. The bank to the right was high, the other looked fifty yards away.

"Can you swim?" he asked her again as he felt the stage being torn sideways by the force of the flood.

"Some, why?"

He never bothered with another word, and pulled her out screaming after him . . .

JAKE LOGAN

SLOCUM AND THE
LADY IN BLUE

J

JOVE BOOKS, NEW YORK

SLOCUM AND THE LADY IN BLUE

A Jove Book / published by arrangement with
the author

PRINTING HISTORY
Jove edition / April 1997

The Putnam Berkley World Wide Web site address is
http://www.berkley.com/berkley

ISBN: 0-515-12049-9

A JOVE BOOK®
Jove Books are published by The Berkley Publishing Group,
200 Madison Avenue, New York, New York 10016.
JOVE and the "J" design are trademarks
belonging to Jove Publications, Inc.

PRINTED IN THE UNITED STATES OF AMERICA

10 9 8 7 6 5 4 3 2 1

SLOCUM AND THE LADY IN BLUE

1

April 1st, 1880.

Rain dripped off the edge of the porch. A gray dawn spread over the mud puddles in the street beyond the parked stagecoach. Two Mexican youths conversed as they hitched the two teams to the tongue. Slocum stood with his shoulder against the building front and drew on the small cigar. His ex-partner had skipped out with his part of a mine sale, and it was not setting well on his stomach. Down to the last puff, he used his finger to flick the butt away in a high arc. He watched the red glow land in the mud and sizzle out.

He shifted the canvas duster on his shoulders, and then reset the high-crown Stetson on his head. The showers were over. From his position on the porch, he could see through the front window inside the stage line office. A tall wiry man in buckskins with a handlebar mustache came from the rear office and crossed the lobby. The man carried a small strongbox in one hand, a double-barrel shotgun in the other.

"Everyone going to Phoenix needs to climb on board," he announced as he crossed the room. "We'll be hauling out in a few minutes."

The attractive woman, wearing a blue-hooded coat that obscured her figure, rose from the bench. Carrying a valise, she came forward behind the driver. Earlier, Slocum had noticed her deep violet eyes and the light brown curls that escaped the hood. Obviously she was no settler's wife, nor a trollop from some house of ill-repute. With a natural interest in any good-looking female, he wondered about her business and destination.

"I certainly hope we have no troubles with bandits or Indians," a small man in a bowler hat said to himself more than to the others as he trailed them. Outside, he paused to press his gold-wire glasses back up his nose, and then blinked at Slocum. "Oh, you're going along too?"

"I hope so," Slocum said as they waited for the driver, who called himself Charlie, to assist the lady in blue up the step and inside the coach.

"Going to Prescott myself," the man under the bowler hat said. "Ernest Meyers is my name."

"Nice to meetcha, Slocum's my name."

"Watch yourself there, fella," the driver said as he steered the shorter man up with a hand on his shoulder. "Don't want anyone hurt loading up."

"Thank you, sir," Meyers said, and took the back seat facing the woman.

"You all right this morning?" Charlie asked. His steel-blue eyes met Slocum's—not a hostile gaze from either party, simply two men sizing up each other.

"Doing fine, Charlie," Slocum said, and climbed inside, sitting down beside Meyers.

The driver closed the door. He made the stage sway as he climbed on the top and settled himself. Above them on the seat, Slocum knew the man was placing the separate lines between his fingers. Control of the horses rested in the man's ability to draw or release the individual lines to the bits.

A shout to his horses and the stage rocked as it took off, the iron rims splitting furrows in the mud. Slocum began to speculate about the woman passenger across from him. However, she acted more interested in viewing the last few buildings as they departed Picket Post than talking with him.

"I hope we don't get stuck this trip," Meyers said.

"I can't recall stages getting stuck much out here," Slocum said, settling back on the upholstered seat.

"Every time it rains—I've been in some real messes."

"Maybe we'll have an uneventful trip," Slocum said, hoping to get a rise from the woman, perhaps learn her name. But she seemed content not to speak with them.

"Where did you say you came from?" Meyers asked.

"I didn't say," Slocum answered. "Actually, I was in Picket Post looking for a man who owes me some money."

"You were looking for a businessman?"

"No, a gambler by the name of Alex Baird. Do you know him?"

"Oh, no, I don't know any gamblers," Meyers said quickly. He folded his arms over his chest and sat up straight. "I sell Bailey's Soap and ladies' care items, like hand mirrors, combs, brushes, and hairpins."

"Must be a real interesting business," Slocum said for lack of anything else to talk to the man about. He was still hoping for a way to bring the woman into their conversation.

"Oh, it was a fine business until the company sent me out here. I'm from Missouri. For five years back there, I had the number-one sales figure for the entire company. Then Mr. Ruppard called me in his office and said, 'Meyers, we need you to go out west in Arizona and New Mexico and sell our famous products out there.' "

"You number one in sales out here?"

"Why, no." Meyers shook his head in disgust. "I'm not even twelfth. Do you know who's number one?"

"No."

"Why, Mr. Ruppard's son-in-law, Philip Long, has my old territory and is number one in the company. Is that a coincidence or what?"

"All I can say is you must have married the wrong woman."

"Oh, no, I've never been married." With a distasteful face, Meyers quickly dismissed any involvement with matrimony in any form.

"Why, he doesn't know all the finer things he's missed, does he, ma'am?" Slocum asked the woman, seeing her about to enter their conversation.

"No. He doesn't," she said, and then withdrew into herself again.

Slocum decided there was nothing he could do to break through the silent facade she presented. A shame too, for he believed she was very attractive behind it all. She remained wrapped in her coat, and wouldn't speak again to them. In her lap was the valise, which she held tightly, as if it was some form of security.

He looked out at the passing hillsides studded with towering saguaros and the deep green greasewood washed by the recent rains that shined in the growing sunshine. The showers were over, and the sun would soon drive the night's chill away. The word he had heard about Baird was that he was probably headed for Prescott. By this time, the rascal had no doubt lost every cent of the proceeds from the mine's sale. Slocum should have known better than to trust Baird as a partner in the first place.

Until he located the scoundrel, he could only lament his losses. Besides, when he did find him, Slocum probably would be no better off money-wise, but at least he would have the satisfaction of a good fistfight. A five-hundred-dollar trouncing was what he had in mind.

They were coming downhill to the first stage stop. He could see the fresh teams harnessed and waiting hip-shot beside the pole corral. Then Slocum blinked for a moment; a man dressed in a business suit, with a carpetbag in hand, stood outside the adobe office with the look of someone waiting for the stage. What was he doing out there?

Overhead, the few gnarled cottonwoods were in early leaf. Their bright green leaves sparkled in the clear air against the red-gray bluffs that rose above the station. Charlie's shouts of "Whoa!" drew the horses into a clattering stop before the depot.

"We ain't going to be here long," he announced, "but you can stretch your legs if you like." He left them to leave the coach on their own, and went off to the office, shedding his fringed gloves and talking privately to a balding man who looked like an agent.

On the ground, Slocum took the opportunity to help the woman down. With a questioning frown, she looked around as she stepped off with his help.

"I suspect it is behind the station," he said under his breath, figuring she wanted the outhouse.

"Thank you," she said, and hurried off in that direction.

"Slocum, this is Harry Johnstone," Meyers said, introducing the new passenger.

"Nice to meet you," Slocum said.

"Who's the lady?" the man asked.

"Damned if I know."

"She certainly is very nice-looking," Meyers added, then looked away, his face becoming red.

"I'd say so," Johnstone agreed.

"She hasn't said but one sentence since we left Picket Post," Slocum added. He raised his arms over his head to stretch the stiffness from his body. Every time he rode a stage, he swore it would be his last time. The cramped quarters and the rough ride always made him as sore as if an old mule had rolled over him.

Their lady in blue rejoined them. Wordless, she greeted them with a bob of her head and passed by to mount the step. Slocum assisted her inside. Then he climbed in and adjusted his gunbelt as he sat beside her.

The other two nodded politely to her as they crawled in and sat across from them. Meyers stabbed his glasses back up his nose. About then Charlie climbed on the stage and gave a shout, and they rolled out for Florence Junction. The woman deliberately kept to her side of the seat and away from Slocum's side. He could recall once riding a stage from Cheyenne to Denver with a voluptuous gal by the name of Ruthie Day. Why, she'd rubbed her hip and leg against him the entire hundred miles. They were both so fired up when they arrived in Denver, they hastily took a room together at the Palace Hotel. Then the two of them went on another uninhibited, bouncy ride on top of the bed that lasted all afternoon. Obviously this woman was no Ruthie Day.

"You're looking for a gambler?" Meyers asked pointedly. "You said you were looking for one?"

"Yes, an Alex Baird," Slocum answered as they were slung from side to side by the ruts.

"I've never heard of him," Johnstone said, gripping the window with his left hand to keep from being tossed further.

The reason Johnstone had never heard of Baird was because the rascal probably wasn't using his real name, Slocum surmised. Why, if *he* owed a man five hundred dollars profit from the sale of a partnership, he'd probably use a different handle too. Filled with a final resolve, Slocum inhaled through his nose and smelled the creosote aroma of the desert and the woman's light perfume. It was time to face reality. He might as well get over his loss and get on with his life. The chances of his ever finding Baird were slim to none. The five hundred dollars was winging away like the purple mourning doves stirred from the road by the coach's approach.

The stage passed through a forest of paloverdes that were emerging in a new coat of green. The crooked stems of the ocatillas topped with red bottle-brush flowers waved in the wind. Slocum and his companions rocked back and forth as they headed for their next stop, Florence Junction.

Finally, with a loud "Whoa!" and the gritty protest of the wooden brake blocks, Charlie locked down the lever and delivered them to their midday stopover.

"They serve a good lunch inside," he announced as he opened the door, removing his floppy hat this time for the woman's sake and helping her to the ground.

Slocum noticed the gray ragged clouds gathering over the Superstitions as he came out of the coach. There would be more rain before the day was over. He followed her in search of the relief station for himself.

She glanced over her shoulder, and her blue eyes looked confused about his purpose. Then she quickly turned back and with her skirt in hand, hurried on. At the outhouses, she looked taken back at the two whitewashed doors, as if in doubt that she should open the one on her side. He reached for the other handle, grateful there were two units.

"Slocum, we need to talk," she said under her breath with a serious gaze at him.

He looked to see how close the others were. The two men were several steps back, but when he turned to her, she was out of sight behind the door. With a shrug, he went in on his side, wondering what she wanted from him as he vented his bladder into the rough-cut oval hole in the bench. What did she need? He listened to his own stream splash somewhere down inside the odorous interior under the floorboards and wondered about the lady in blue.

2

Ralph Moore loathed even being inside the dirty shack that stank of sour socks and other odors that he didn't even want to think about. The bunks were unmade. Tattered remains of blankets were thrown back and left as they had been when their lazy tenants had climbed from under them. The small glazed windows so filthy with dirt and cobwebs that he couldn't see through them.

The table was buried under a filthy pile of crockery and metal utensils covered with wasted food and congealed egg yolk. A tall pack rat had welcomed his entry into the cabin. To show his spite, the rodent had stood on his hind feet and dined on the remains of a biscuit. For a full fifteen seconds Moore had come within inches of blasting the nasty whiskered rodent to hell, but he'd considered the damage that such a shot would inflict on the cabin, and had merely bellowed at the critter. It had left in haste.

Ralph Moore considered himself an educated man, and having to deal with persons like Bobbie Gates and the rest of his gang of thugs was more at times than he could stomach. He had purposely purchased this two-bit ranch and recorded the deed in a dead man's name so he would have a place for these misfits to stay.

Seated on a straight-back chair, far enough away from the bunks so no biting bedbugs could leap on him, and with enough room to kill any rat that charged him, he waited for the gang's return. They were supposed to have hit the stage station the night before and run off the stock.

He held a healthy bank note on the Pinal-Maricopa Stage Line. The operation could make money if he owned and operated it, especially with his management skills. Had the gang done anything? Rain the night before might have messed them up, but it also would have been the ideal time to strike. Hell, blame it on the damn Apaches. But Bobbie Gates wasn't the sharpest individual, and the men surrounding him had less sense.

At the sound of horses, Moore rose and went out on the narrow porch. The gang rode up looking like five refugees from a border army. Bobbie wore a big Mexican sombrero— Ralph figured that the rat-faced man considered himself some kind of Mexican general. Carlos was a sleepy Mexican, Coy and Lafferty were both halfbreeds, and Two Feathers claimed to be a full-blood Apache, but he wasn't. Still, for the moment they suited his needs, and with this isolated ranch for their headquarters, he could direct them to handle his business.

"Did you scatter them stage-line horses?" he asked without even a hello.

"Hell, no, the rain came and we didn't want to be tracked back here." In cocky fashion, Bobbie pushed the sombrero to the back of his head and then dismounted. In his shotgun chaps he waded stiffly to the foot of the porch. "We don't want to hang. Do you?"

"I wanted. . . ." He caught himself and frowned at the dull-faced gang members sitting on their horses. Then he motioned over his first in command. They walked off a short distance from the others, and after he felt certain their conversation would be private, he began to talk to his man.

"No more stage-line business for a while. We've got another problem. You know that ranch with the mine, the Spanish land grant in the Superstitions?"

"Yeah, we took you there once. Hell, I won't have that place. Them damn Apaches are all over that damn place and they'll sure kill you."

"Listen to me. A woman showed up this week and her name is Betty Wells. Somehow she bought out this Don DeVaga, and she has a deed to the whole thing."

"Where is she?" Bobbie asked, his sour breath so bad that it forced Ralph to turn his face for a moment to escape the odor.

"This morning I understand she intended to take a stage from Picket Post on her way to Goldfield. I think she's going to try to hire someone to lead her to the ranch."

"Who's she going to hire?"

"How the hell should I know? You get up there and find out what she's doing, and send word to me as soon as you learn anything. We need that ranch title if we're ever going to open and work that Iron Mountain mine. And as soon as the stupid U.S. Army gets them blanket-ass Indians out of those mountains, I want that mine operating."

"Yeah, I know. What does she look like?"

"Tall, light brown hair, blue eyes—she's very attractive. She looks nothing like any woman you'd see on the frontier. She wears a long blue coat with a damn hood. Hell, there ain't nothing but whores up at Goldfield. You won't miss her."

"What do we do with her?"

"Be a shame if those Indians got hold of her," Ralph said slyly. "And maybe raped her until they got tired of her and then they killed her with a hatchet."

"Why let the gawdamn Indians do that to her if she looks that good?"

"Do it yourself to her then—" Ralph drew his breath through his nose for composure. This man's stupidity was more than he could bear at times.

"We get her out of the way, can you scatter the stage line's horses?" Ralph asked.

"No, not while they can track us back here. We'll do that as soon as it's dried out." Then Bobbie shook his head in disbelief. "What makes you think this woman will even want to stay on that ranch?"

"She won't even consider my best offer. She said something about going to see the place first, then she'd decide if she wanted to sell it. I don't want her to decide a gawdamn thing. You understand me?"

"Sure. How did she ever get the deed?"

"Bobbie, I said I didn't know, but her papers are all in order. Some big law firm in Washington, D.C., represented her and fixed them better than any I'd ever seen. That's why it is best she never comes back from her first visit." Ralph looked hard at his foreman. "I want her killed and no excuses."

"I hear, yeah."

Ralph counted out the double eagles from his vest into Bobbie's hand. Forty bucks a month per hand, and sixty for Bobbie, was high wages even for cutthroats, but it earned their loyalty. Still, if the Iron Mountain Mine produced gold the way the assay report said it would, this outlay would be nothing. No frilly society girl was going to steal away his best prospect to settle his accounts and become rich as well.

He was lucky that he had not already brought that old man from Sonora to sign the deed as the verified last heir of DeVaga. With the girl out of the way and things calmer, he could proceed with his original plan. Now he watched Bobbie go to each man and pay him his wages. The smiles of the simpleton army were enough for him. He had other business to do this day.

"We'll find her," Gates promised, and Ralph struck out for his sorrel horse hitched to the corral. Surely they could manage to kill one city girl and some stupid guide she'd hire at Goldfield. Besides, he had another matter to attend to this day.

The long shadows from the towering red spheres lay across the valley. Ralph let the sorrel drop off the mountainside on the game trail. On the flat, he corrected his course and reined the horse for the unpainted ranch house in the cottonwoods that lined the small watercourse.

He dismounted at the hitch rail in front of the clapboard residence. No one was in sight, but a friendly Scotch collie barked at the side of the house. Then the dog retreated to the back porch, satisfied that no one threatening had arrived.

"Evening, Mary," Ralph said, removing his hat in the doorway.

In her thirties and tall, with a long neck that she tried to hide with high collars on her dresses, she stood at the dishpan. Her familiar figure and the turn of her long hip under the calico dress stirred him as he hung his hat on the peg. Her brown hair was brushed and shone as she dried her hands from the dish washing. She acknowledged him with a nod and a hard swallow.

"I guess you're in a hurry?" she asked with her head bent down as she hung the towel on a bar.

"Not that big of a one," he said, removing his suit coat and hanging it beside his Stetson. Then he crossed the room and inspected the cookstove.

"This from supper?" he asked of the remaining food.

"Yes."

"Why, Mary Clayton, aren't you pleased to see me?" He picked up a cold biscuit from the nearby pan and placed a browned piece of cold steak in the center. Then, as deliberately as he could, he stood a few feet from her with his boots planted apart.

"You know how much the ranch payment is?" He took a large bite of the sandwich and waited for her reply.

"Yes," she said, subdued.

"Then why don't you pull my boots off to start with?" He dropped on a chair and extended his high-top handmade black boots toward her. She lugged off the first one. He rearranged the biscuit to keep from losing it, and then let her lift the right one before taking another bite.

"Saving the ranch, aren't we?" he asked.

"Yes."

"Why, taking off that boot sure feels really good, Mary. You ever get real relief like that?"

"I don't know." She shook her head, acting confused as she stood before him. The boot in hand, she stepped back a few feet and stood like a statue. Then she dropped it with a thud.

He rose and moved closer to her. She started to back up, but he caught her roughly by the arm and made her stay. Then he began to undo the buttons on her dress, one at a time. She gasped for air as each one came open. Finally he forced her to hold her shoulders back so her pear-shaped breasts were exposed. The dark nipples hardened and pointed when exposed to the room air. He eyed them, consumed with greed to have her. He slipped the dress off her, staying her arms from clutching herself as he studied his prize.

With his short breath raging from his mouth, he dragged her to the large bed in the corner and shoved her down on the mattress. In a flash, his pants were open and her legs were roughly parted. He climbed on top of her and thrust himself inside of her. She stifled a cry as he forced himself in deeper; the bed protested under them.

"Mary's making another ranch payment, isn't she?" he asked, out of breath as he drove deeper and deeper into her.

There was no answer. Her face was turned aside on the pillow as she avoided looking up at him while he continued his attack.

"You're making a payment now, aren't you, Mary?" he huffed.

"Yes, I am!" she finally screamed into his face. "Are you satisfied?"

"Yes, now I am." A smile crossed his face. *And you'll make many more payments to me, little lady.*

Under the starlight, ready to leave for Picket Post, Ralph checked the cinch on his saddle. Satisfied he had done all he could with her for one night, he swung in the saddle and reined up the gelding. Mary had gone to the bunkhouse for her two children. The two cowboys who worked for her kept them for her on the last day of the month—when he came by and took his ranch payment.

Sure a shame Enos Clayton had been killed in that horse accident two years before. The young rancher had left poor Mary with a five-hundred-dollar note on their ranch. She'd tried to work out the repayment without success, until Ralph had told her that the time was up.

The first time he took her lanky body was on top of the great walnut desk in his office. Yes, Mary would make many more payments to him. He spurred the sorrel down the valley, still smiling to himself.

3

"I don't need anything to eat, Mr. Slocum," she said to dismiss his concern as they stood outside the Florence Junction stage stop under the palm frond porch. Acting unsettled, she looked around as if speaking to him brought some great risk that he could not fathom. He could do without a meal, especially stage-station fare. Besides, he was interested in what she wanted of him.

"My name is Betty Wells." She compressed her lips as if considering whether to go on or not.

"We're alone here. What can I do for you?" he asked.

"You may consider me very forward but I . . ." She stopped as a Mexican youth passed them on his way inside. The boy gone, she continued in a guarded voice. "I fear my life is in danger, and I also think you are probably the only one who can help me."

He frowned. "Why didn't you go to the sheriff back at Picket Post if you're in danger from someone?"

"Oh, Mr. Slocum, I don't know anyone in this land and the people I have met . . ." She dropped her shoulders in defeat under the blue coat.

"Who's after you?"

"Do you know a banker in Picket Post by the name of Moore?"

"No, ma'am, never met the man. Is he after you?"

She closed her eyes and shook her head. "All I can say is that man is no gentleman." Then she gave a great sigh before continuing. "I was told all the men in the West would respect a woman. I mean—anyway, why am I telling you all this?"

"Because you said you needed some help."

"Yes, I do." She swallowed to recover her composure.

"That's settled. Where are you going?" he asked, hoping to learn something more about her problems and make some sense of it all.

"Goldfield. I own a ranch near there."

"That's a mining town. There are no ranches near there that I know about. The Apaches, or at least the Yavapais, are on the warpath up and down the Salt River and the mountains all around there." He knew that from his own experience. A few years earlier, he'd dealt cards at the Red Horse Saloon for several months during the winter, and Goldfield was not a cow town.

"I own the DeVaga land grant of six thousand acres."

"I never heard of it. But I'm afraid you might just as well own a share of Hell." He shook his head ruefully over her admission. He didn't care if she owned the whole territory of Arizona; where she was speaking of going was hostile Indian country, worthless to do anything with—unless she hired a private army.

"If you don't want to help me—"

"I didn't say that. It is just going to be damn difficult to make much out of your claim."

"There is a ranch headquarters. I at least want to see it."

He could tell by the set of her firm chin that she had her mind made up about examining this place of hers. This woman had no idea what brutal renegade Indians did to their victims, especially attractive victims. From under the edge of the porch, he studied the growing cloud bank over the Superstitions. It would be raining by the time they swung around the face of the mountain range and headed for Goldfield.

"Can I hire you?" she asked.

"To do what?"

"To take me to the ranch. I know I might not be able to stay there, but I want to see it."

"I guess, but you have to go by my rules. So when and if I decide to turn back for safety reasons, you listen to me." He waited for her answer.

"You want to be the boss?"

"Yes, because I don't want to become a victim."

"I can't argue with that. How much a day do you cost, sir?"

"That depends on how dangerous it gets."

"Mr. Slocum!" She drew her head back and looked peeved at him. "How will I know if I can afford you?"

"You can," he said softly as the others came out of the station.

"You two ain't eating?" Meyers asked, pushing his glasses back to his face as he came out of the depot.

"No, we got kinda queasy with all that rocking around," Slocum said to the man.

"Oh, this trip ain't bad. I came from Tucson one time and the Apaches—sorry, ma'am. I didn't mean to bring up bad things before a lady."

"Go right ahead, Mr. Meyers. I am certain I have heard worse things," she said as Slocum helped her back into the coach.

"These Apaches came screaming out of this wash and soon their arrows were flying around inside the stage."

"Where were you at, man?" Johnstone asked as they all were seated again.

"Why, down on the floor, of course."

His reply drew some laughter.

"What's so funny? What would *you* do?" the man asked, looking bewildered at their amusement.

"Probably gotten under you," Slocum said, and shook his head, still amused at the indignation of the drummer.

Charlie rushed out of the building wearing a long-tail yellow slicker, and climbed on the box after checking that everyone was aboard. With a shout, they were on their way to Goldfield. A rumble of thunder swept across the land of catclaw. The high bank of clouds cut off the sun, and Slocum figured that soon they would be in the shield of rain advancing on them.

Each man busied himself tying down the canvas curtains in preparation. It was a job that could have been more easily accomplished at the stopover, but they made progress between the pitch and roll of the coach. The woman did the one beside her, and then they sat back in the darkened interior as the wind picked up.

"There's the rain," Johnstone said as the drumming became louder on the roof.

"I surely hope we don't get stuck," Meyers said aloud, and raised his glance to the ceiling.

"How many times you ever been stuck?" Johnstone asked.

"Too many times. You have to get out in the mud and get a hold of a wheel and push until you fall on your face in the stuff."

Slocum sat back and listened to two men banter over the roar of the increasing storm and the noise of the coach and horses. Charlie, above them, shouted to his leaders; he never slacked his speed in the rain since the road was not too rough.

Betty Wells was her name. He knew that much, and that she owned the DeVaga Ranch. He'd never heard of it. There were lots of ranches he had never heard of, but for a lone woman to own so much land, even if it was mostly cactus and prickly pear, was unusual. And how did someone from the East, and a female on top of that, ever become the titleholder. Then there was her cussed determination to see this place— why, it probably had been burned out and gutted like most of the other outposts in the territory. She simply did not know the destructive force of the Apaches. They had scorched the land despite the Army's best efforts. And the broken mountain ranges between Four Peaks and the Superstitions were the ideal places to avoid if one wanted to go on breathing.

Rain dripped and leaked in past their curtains as it pounded harder on the roof and sides. Charlie's shouts to his horses were almost lost in the storm's roar. But the driver kept moving, slicing through some dry washes that Slocum peeked out at. The washes were already several inches deep in floodwater. If the rains kept up, they might be lucky to reach their destination. Downpours like this filled the normally dry arroyos and often caused serious flooding.

Lightning crashed close by, and Betty Wells bolted upright. When she settled on the seat, her hip was familiarly against Slocum's for the first time. The thunder grew closer and more intense, and he wondered if Charlie could even see anything in the deluge. They pitched going downhill, and Charlie shouted for the horses to run.

"What's he doing?" Meyers asked, holding his hands over his ears and clinching his eyes shut.

"He's making a run to cross a wash, I guess," Slocum shouted.

She looked with alarm at him. Protectively he put his arm around her shoulder. She didn't object. There was no way to see a thing, but he could hear the horses splashing in lots of water, and he could feel the coach being taken sideways by the force of the stream.

"We're all going to die!" Meyers shouted.

"What do you think we should do?" the lady asked in a subdued voice.

"Stay with me," Slocum said. "Can you swim?"

"Will we have to?"

"I don't know."

The horses were screaming in a panic Slocum recognized as desperation. He rose and opened the door to see outside. Water lapped at the floor of the coach. There wouldn't be much time to make a good decision. They were stopped in a choppy sea of fast-rising water. The bank to the right was high, the other looked fifty yards away.

"Can you swim?" he asked her again as he felt the stage being torn sideways by the force of the flood.

"Some, why?"

He never bothered with another word, and pulled her out screaming after him. In the rushing stream he was well over his head, and his boots soon were filled with water. Unable to recover it, he grimaced as his hat was gone fast, bobbing on the waves. He treaded water, and watched her blue coat spread over the surface as she gave another loud scream at the shock of the cold water soaking through her clothing. To his relief, she began to paddle—she could swim some.

"Keep swimming," he shouted, anxious to stay close to her in the raging current. What was so damn valuable that she had to hold onto that valise?

The rain blinded him as they were swept downstream. In a flash of blinding lightning, he saw the stage topple over, and heard the anguished screams of the panicked horses being pulled in by the roaring flood. Somewhere Meyers and Johnstone were both yelling for help. There was no way he could help them—he'd be lucky to save the lady and himself.

Slocum took her hand and then he kicked for the shore. She wasn't doing a bad job of staying afloat for a fully clothed woman. Others would have already drowned with the lead weight of their soaked clothing. Not paying attention, he took in a muddy mouthful from a high wave and was ducked under, but even as the force sped them further downstream, he knew she was a strong-willed person.

Out of breath and coughing up phlegm, they waded out of the flood. He watched for a sign of the others. He hoped they had not all drowned, but this far down the wash, there was no indication any of the others had survived. Then he spotted Meyers splashing his arms and legs and screaming to be saved. With a grim nod at the pale-faced Betty on the bank, Slocum waded out to direct the hysterical man to shore.

"Where's Johnstone?" he asked when he caught the drummer's hand.

"Sitting on the stagecoach last I seen him." Meyers went to choking up water and heaving for his breath.

"You seen Charlie?" Slocum asked, dragging the staggering man into the shallows.

"No, I ain't seen anyone. This is the last straw, I'm quitting this job." Meyers stomped his foot in protest.

"Whatever you say," Slocum said, looking out over the water for any sign of the other two. Rivulets poured down his face; he had for certain lost his hat in the swim, and his hair was plastered down on his forehead.

"Are the others drowned?" she asked, taking a hold of Slocum's wet sleeve when he came out to stand beside her.

"I haven't seen a sign of them and the water's getting deeper by the minute," he said as they backed up. Where were Johnstone and the driver? No telling. The rushing flood was thick with mud and the darkness of the storm hindered his vision.

"What will we do next?" she asked with a shiver.

"Build a fire and dry out if we can. We're about midway between both stage stops and these dry washes off the face of the Superstitions will all be flooded. Not much we can do until they go down except wait.''

"How long will that be?'' she asked.

"Maybe a couple of hours or even a day.''

"How are we going to start a fire in this?'' Meyers asked, about to cry with rain washing down his face.

"I guess gather some dry wood,'' Slocum said as he sat down on the ground to empty the water from his boots.

4

The fire crackled, and his boots were upside down on sticks beside him. He wiggled his toes in his drying socks as they all sat studying the flames. The clearing sky was filled with bright stars. The flickering blue-red blaze of the ironwood lit the darkness, and shone on her handsome face as Slocum wondered about Betty Wells.

"We're lucky to be alive," she said over the rush of the nearby flooding wash. "I'm grateful to you, sir."

"Just something that had to be done," Slocum said. "Everything all right in that valise you brought along?"

"Oh, yes, its fine. But you, you've lost your good hat and heaven knows what else in your efforts to save us. Isn't that so, Mr. Meyers?"

"Ah, yes, it is," the small man said, sitting in huddled dejection. "I'm quitting the Bailey Soap Company. There are other companies that would appreciate my services. I'm going back to Missouri and sell something else."

"Maybe sell women's undergarments," Slocum said to get a rise from the prudish little man.

"Oh, no."

"I'm certain a man of your vast experience can get any job

he wants," she said with a private frown for Slocum at his comment.

"Just trying to help," Slocum said to her.

"How are we going to sleep out here, Slocum?" Meyers asked.

"I guess on the ground."

"Hmm," the man said, and rose to his feet, looking out into the desert as if seeking some lighted place of privacy for his own relief.

"Nothing out there will bother you." Slocum said to reassure the man.

"I'll be right back."

"Certainly," Slocum said, grateful for his absence. He watched the man cautiously shuffle off into the greasewood as if expecting to find a bear.

"What about Charlie and Johnstone?" Betty asked.

"No idea. Come dawn, we'll head upstream for the road, and by then they'll surely have some help here for us. I can't figure what happened to those two. They never went by us swimming anyway."

"It's strange to be thirsty beside a rushing river."

"Pretty muddy for drinking right now. It should be running clear enough to drink some by first light."

"Good. You recall me keeping you from eating at Florence Junction?"

"Yes," he said, amused.

"I wish now that we'd eaten when we had the chance."

"I agree," he said, hugging his knees. "All we have to do is make it until sunup and they'll surely be here looking for us."

The lonely yip of a coyote carried across the desert floor. The woman twisted to pinpoint the source. Slocum knew it was somewhere across the wash and nearly a quarter mile away. Despite the plaintive howling, they were in no danger.

"Help! Help! There's a wolf out here! My God, we'll be eaten alive!" Meyers came screaming as he fell over clumps of greasewood, then scrambled to his feet like a madman. Out of breath, he came charging into the campfire's light.

"Rest easy, Meyers. If we keep the fire up, he'll stay on his own ground."

"You got your gun?" the man asked, checking all around.

"Sure."

"Good, then you can kill him."

"I guess so," Slocum said, but he felt certain the water-doused ammunition was probably no good.

"I wish we had some food." Meyers looked around dejectedly.

"We don't."

"Are you going to watch the fire?"

"I'll handle it." Slocum grew wary of the man's unabated questions, and was relieved when Meyers finally stretched out on his side and looked ready to go to sleep.

"He means nothing by it," she said quietly over the crackling logs that gave off a starburst of small sparks into the red ashes.

"I know. He just drives me mad at times."

"I can see that. Where do you live?" she asked, seated close beside Slocum.

"Wherever I plant my butt." He chuckled and shook his head at the situation. "I usually say where I hang my hat, but I don't have one of those left."

"Who are you, Slocum?" She never looked in his direction, but stared ahead at the fire.

"The guy that your mother told you to watch out for."

"What do you do for a living?"

"You name it. Deal cards, prospect, scout for the Army, herd sheep, cattle."

She stretched her arms over her head and yawned. "I think there is a lot you've left out telling me."

"No reason to. See, there are some things that you can't ever redo. No matter if it isn't the truth, it follows you. Things that should have been straightened out years ago and didn't get taken care of right, they come back to haunt a person."

"Why don't you—"

"It's way too late to change the outcome." He turned to look into her eyes, which reflected the fire's light. Slowly he leaned toward her until their lips finally met and he began to taste the lust of a real woman. They slipped into each other's arms, and the heady power swept through him as he savored the honey of her mouth. Only their damp clothes separated them. They finally sat up and sought a moment of recovery.

She drew her face back in shock and sucked in a deep breath. "I'm married."

He sat up straight to recover his composure, then tossed a handful of twigs on the fire, and they were consumed in a flare of light.

What else did he expect?

The quarter moon rose over the dark wall of the Superstitions. He'd finally convinced her to go to sleep on the ground under his duster. Meyers snored on the other side of him. Slocum's eyes burned from lack of sleep as he rose to his feet and tried to work out the stiffness. He knew little more about the woman, aside from the fact that she expected him to deliver her to some ruin of a ranch in the mountains. If they didn't get an arrow shaft in their backsides, they'd be lucky. Stars overhead filled the sky with pinpricks of light and cast a pearl glow over the desert.

He rose quietly and moved off at a distance to relieve himself. Baird was gone with his money, and Mrs. Wells was up there sleeping sound enough for one who was no doubt unaccustomed to the ground as her mattress. He drew in a deep breath. She was some woman.

Where in hell was her husband? Why wasn't he out there helping her? What kind of a man left his wife at the mercy of bastards like this banker Moore and the entire Apache nation, not to mention stage wrecks. If they ever met, he planned to kick the sorry rascal's butt. His own business completed out in the greasewood, he walked back to the sleeping pair.

On his haunches, he worked to rebuild the fire. The radiant heat was going down, and both of his wards needed more warmth as dawn drew near. The coldest portion of the day in the desert was fast approaching. He watched to the east as he piled the longer chunks on top of the main flames. He would be grateful when the sun peeked over the great wall. Help for them must be on the way, unless they were cut off by more floods between there and Goldfield.

5

Meyers and the woman awoke with the dawn, both sitting up hugging their arms, cold and groggy. Slocum started them marching upstream toward the road. They staggered along half asleep. A half mile from their camp they rounded a bend and spotted the stagecoach lying on its side in the wash. It looked like a chocolate-coated toy, mud-wrapped and piled high with debris from the flood.

"Should we look in it?" she asked.

"You two stay here. I'll wade over there," he said, and then sat down on the high ground to remove his stiff boots. He needed to look inside and also get their personal things from the boot. His purpose in removing his boots was to save his footgear from the knee-deep stream slicing through the sloppy wash bed between him and the stage.

"I don't see any bodies," Meyers offered, standing on his toes.

"If they aren't in the coach, they could be washed down to the Colorado by now," Slocum said as he started for the disabled vehicle on exposed soles across the pointed rocks and sticks.

"Be careful you don't sink in that sand," she said, concerned. "They warned me there is sand out here in the West that will suck you under."

"Quicksand, they call it." He glanced back at her worried face. "In a river maybe, but not out here." Then, as he winced at something sharp underfoot, his bare feet began to sink into the cold mud, and he was forced to raise them individually with effort from the sucking goo; he finally crossed the calf-deep water and reached the coach. He undid the canvas ribbons on the upper side of the rear boot. Then he reached in, felt around, and finally drew out a dripping valise.

"This yours?" he asked her as she stood on the bank.

"No, that must be Johnstone's."

Slocum put it on top of the upturned wheel. Determined to find their luggage, he undid more ties and came out with another badly mud-stained bag.

"That's mine and there is a millinery box too," she said.

Hell only knew what a woman's hat would look like after going through such a flood, he decided, and parted the canvas more and looked inside for the box. There were two other cases; no doubt they were the drummer's. He hauled them out, and Meyers called out, "Yes, that's mine."

On the third try, he found her hat box, and she clapped her hands. He grinned at her and then drew a deep breath; the mud and water on his feet and shins were cold. When all the cargo was piled on top of the wheel and the side of the up-turned coach, he sloshed around to the middle and then crawled up on the coach to look down inside the compartment.

From his perch, he could see a body inside. The mud-painted corpse of Johnstone was nestled on the bottom. It had little likeness to the living man; he had become a victim of the wreck and the flooding.

"Johnstone didn't make it," he said with a wry shake of his head.

"He's dead?" Meyers asked, as if he couldn't believe the fact.

"Yes, and I'm going to need your help to get him out."

"What can I do?" Meyers shouted.

"Take your shoes off and come help me get his body out," Slocum said, almost impatient with the man's hesitation.

"Can't we leave him for the stage people?"

"No! Get over here."

"Well I can't see why—" Meyers went to babbling to himself as he removed his shoes.

"I'll go," she said.

"Oh, no, this ain't no place for a lady," the drummer said. "I'll do it—ouch! What was that I stepped on? Glass?" He stopped and, standing on one leg, turned up his muddy sole to examine it. "I think this whole thing should be the stage line's business."

"Come on, Meyers!" Slocum waved for the man to get over there. Then, shaking his head, he lowered himself into the coach to wait for the drummer to come help him. He bent over and lifted Johnstone's rigid body under the arms until it was upright. But with the dead man bent slightly at the waist, there was no way for him to get the slippery clay-coated corpse out the door overhead.

"What am I to do?" Meyers asked from the top side of the coach.

"Reach in and get ahold of his clothes or something and I'll boost him up to you."

"I never handled a dead man. Oh, my God!"

Slocum looked up, and the man was wringing his hands in some sort of uncontrollable rage. Pale as a sheet, he looked ready to puke up his entire intestinal tract. Then he shot forward, and that was what he did over the underside of the carriage—vomited away.

"The sooner we get this done—" Slocum's words were cut

off by more coughing and barfing. Let him get it all up and perhaps it would be over, Slocum figured. Handling dead men never was an easy thing; some folks were more squeamish than others.

"I guess it's over," the drummer huffed, looking at Slocum again—even paler than before.

"Here," Slocum said, wrestling with the slick muddy form to get it up. Obviously the little man was some help, for the body was soon going out the door overhead more easily than Slocum could manage by himself.

"He's come alive! Help me!" Meyers fell over the side, screaming at the top of his lungs.

Slocum surfaced from the coach, using both arms to push himself up and swinging his legs over the side. There was no way Johnstone was alive, but when he looked down in the stream, there on his back was Meyers, pinned under the muddy dead man. The squalling drummer was flailing his legs and arms with water going everywhere.

"He's dead!" Slocum jumped down and pulled the body aside. "Get hold of yourself, man!"

"Oh, I swear that he took hold of me and pushed me down in this mud." Meyers half rose, shaking like someone who had seen the devil; then he lost his footing and took another bath in the slimy stream.

Coated in mud from the corpse and from Meyers's cavorting, Slocum took the dead man by the collar and dragged him across to the far bank.

"I could have helped you. Poor Johnstone, what a shame," Betty said under her breath, coming down to where Slocum had left the body on dry land.

"I know you could have helped," he said, not wanting to even talk about it. He turned and went back across the wash for the rest of their things.

Meyers was slipping and sliding in his return, carrying one

of his own cases on his back. As they passed by each other, Meyers fell face-down under his load and rained more mud all over Slocum. Without a word, he hoisted the protesting drummer up by the collar and, his case in the other hand, carried both to shore, where he unceremoniously deposited them.

"Now stay here!" He looked at the clear azure sky for help before he started back for the rest of the things. Soon all their things were finally piled on the beach. The chore completed, he sat on a case and shook his head in disbelief.

"You should see yourself," she said, holding her chin and observing him. Her smile taunted him.

"I can imagine," he said with a sigh.

"Are we going to have to bury him?" Meyers asked.

"I guess so. There isn't an undertaker at Goldfield."

"How we going to do that?"

"There's usually a shovel strapped on a stage," Slocum said, pushing off his knees to stand up. "If it ain't washed away, I'll go over there and get it."

"And you just came from there," she said, turning quickly away to hide her amusement at the situation. If he hadn't been so mad, he'd have laughed too as he waded through the cold mess to reach the stage again.

"This ground's hard as a rock," Meyers complained, standing in the knee-deep grave. They'd taken turns digging.

"Then you can bring rocks over to pile on him," Slocum said, dropping his latest ones on the pile.

"I just don't see why the stage line doesn't have to bury him."

"Maybe we can send them a bill for doing it," Slocum said, and started back for more rocks.

"What's wrong?" Betty asked, coming with several smaller stones.

"He wants the stage line to pay us for the funeral expenses."

"Will they do that?"

"Lord, I have no idea. Poor man needs to be planted and it's all we can do for him." Slocum wiped his face on his dirty sleeve and then shook his head. "Get him buried, we can set out on foot for Goldfield. I can't believe that they haven't sent anyone out here to check on us."

"It can't go much deeper," Meyers said.

"Good, quit digging. We'll cover him with rocks."

"It's too hard to dig."

"I said get the hell out here and help us get enough rocks!"

"Sure," the appalled little man said, and climbed out on his knees. "I just wanted to tell you—"

"Slocum is a little upset at the moment," the lady said to Meyers. "Just help us get more rocks. He'll be fine, if we give him time."

"All I wanted to do—"

But the disapproving shake of her head quieted the drummer.

Slocum dragged the dead man's body up close to the open grave. On his knees, he removed Johnstone's wallet and searched it, finding a water-soaked card reading: "Harold Johnstone, Senior Examiner, Department of Banking, Territory of Arizona. 103 Lincoln St., Prescott, Arizona Territory." What was he doing getting on at a stage outpost? There was no bank there. Slocum looked at the folded money, mostly singles, no fortune, hardly more than travel funds.

"What do we know about him?" Betty asked, bringing more rocks to dump on the stack.

"He was a bank examiner," Slocum said, pushing himself up. "Isn't that strange?"

"No," she said. "I thought I saw him a few days ago in

Moore's bank. But I never saw him face to face until he got on the stage.''

''Anyway, this and some change is all I can find to send his next of kin.'' He handed her the wallet to look at as Meyers arrived with another armload of stones.

''That's enough,'' Slocum said, satisfied that they could bury the poor man with what material they had on hand. With Meyers's help, they placed the dead man in the hole and then climbed out.

''Maybe a word should be said.'' Slocum looked over at them, but both had bowed their heads, leaving him the task.

''Lord, we're sending you Harold Johnstone. Through no fault of his, he's heading your way. Open the gates and receive him as one of yours. Amen.''

''Amen.''

''Now all three of you raise your hands to the sky!'' someone ordered, and the hair on the back of Slocum's neck rose. He knew that voice from somewhere.

6

"Well, what have we here?" the big lawman asked, waving his pistol around as he stepped in and drew Slocum's from his holster. "Guess your little trick to rob the stage didn't work. What did you do, kill him to cut the split?" He indicated the dead man.

"What in the hell are you talking about, Jim Crawford?" Slocum demanded.

"That is you, Slocum, under all that mud? I'd never thought a fancy fella like you ever got dirty. Hmm, sure sorry I broke up your little scheme here to steal the strongbox."

"Talk sense! We were swept away in a damn flood yesterday. We don't have any strongbox. Now this is enough of this foolishness. This poor man was drowned and whatever happened to the driver Charlie, we don't know." A year before this blustering lawman with the tin star the size of Texas had been little more than a flunky around Goldfield. His huge size made him all the more ominous to the little man and Betty, but Slocum wasn't afraid of him, except for the fact that he had the drop on them.

"Who's she?" Crawford asked, still looking hard at the three of them.

"Betty Wells, she's from—"

"Philadelphia," she put in. "And I see no reason—"

"Just keep your hands up until I figure this out." He motioned toward them with the muzzle of his Colt. His gun pointed at them, he knelt down and looked in the hole as if trying to ascertain the dead man's identity.

"Who's he?"

"Bank examiner from Prescott, Harold Johnstone."

"Stay there," Crawford warned. "You three are under arrest until that strongbox is recovered. There is too much here unanswered."

"What's the charges?"

"Stage robbing and maybe murder."

"Crawford, I'm tempted to take one of these rocks and bust your head in. We have been without food for near a day. We almost drowned in a flood, and you have audacity to—"

"Stay there, Slocum, or I'll plug daylight through your gut!"

"Don't tempt him," Betty said, pulling on Slocum's sleeve.

He knew what he would do if he was by himself—he'd have already killed the worthless Crawford and left him for the buzzards. The danger to her was the only thing that forced him to remain in control.

"Who the hell are you?" Crawford demanded of the drummer.

"Meyers—Ernest Meyers—B-B-Bailey's Soap salesman."

"What part did you play in this robbery?" Crawford demanded, shoving the gun's muzzle in the wide-eyed man's face.

"Part?" Meyers began to tremble and fell to his knees. His hands went together as he began to pray.

"Leave him alone!"

"Mind your own damn business, Slocum. I think he'll tell me the truth when I get through with him."

"What's going on here?" a man dressed in a suit demanded as he rode up on a big horse. Several others came with him and sat their mounts.

"I've got the damn stage robbers. This little one's about to piss in his pants and he's going to tell me where the money is, Mr. Fisher."

"Crawford! Let that man go!" Fisher ordered, and dismounted in haste. He crossed the space between horse and lawman in long strides.

"No," Crawford said, roughly dragging Meyers to his feet by a sleeve. "I aim to beat the truth out of this little roach!"

"Let him go," the man said, throwing his arms in between the lawman and Meyers until he wrestled Crawford's hold loose.

Crawford staggered back and then stopped, teetering on his boot heels. He was out of breath and his eyes held the wild look of a madman. Fisher spoke softly to the man as Slocum and the woman took Meyers aside and comforted the poor babbling drummer.

Slocum only half-heard the man's introduction.

"I'm Garnet Fisher, agent for the Maricopa-Pinal stage line at Goldfield, Mister . . ."

"Slocum," he said, his gaze still on the lawman, who sulked a few yards away. "You better tell Crawford that he's lucky to be alive."

"I'm sorry. He gets a little zealous at times. What happened?"

"The stage was wrecked in a flood. Charlie misjudged it and drove off in too deep a water."

"I'm surprised. He was a very experienced driver. Did he survive?"

"I don't know. This man Johnstone was drowned. Meyers, the woman, and I managed to swim out."

"Lucky that you three survived from the looks of things.

This gulch roared big from the watermarks on things. Is the stage strongbox on the coach?''

"I have no idea. We got the dead man out and our personal things. I never looked up in the front boot."

"Some of you look the coach over," he said to the men who'd came with him. "Mr. Slocum has not seen the strong-box. If it's not there, then start riding this wash until we find it. There's a hundred-dollar reward for its recovery."

"Guess there's a lot of money in it," Slocum said.

"A thousand dollars perhaps. And ma'am. I am sorry for any inconvenience. I'm Garnet Fisher with the stage line." He swept his hat off.

"Betty Wells, and this is Ernest Meyers."

"May I apologize to both of you. Marshal Crawford gets a little carried away at times with his authority."

"I had hoped the driver had managed to cut the teams loose and survive," she said. "We thought the horses might have escaped and run to Goldfield."

"No, ma'am, they never came in. I guess they must have been swept away too. We thought all night that Charlie had held the stage at Florence Junction because of the storm. See, the telegraph was down too. Then when they fixed the thing this morning, they said he had started out. We figured the stage had been wrecked or robbed."

She nodded.

"I have a buckboard coming for three of you. Are you all right, Mr. Meyers?"

The drummer nodded woodenly as he stood beside her look-ing crestfallen and even shorter. Slocum had swept up his own revolver, and brushed off the grit on it with an angry glare in the direction of the lawman, who had waded out to the coach to help the others search for the box.

"Here's the dead man's wallet," he said, handing it to the agent.

"Thanks again, Slocum. I'm sorry about the mixup. Marshal Crawford meant nothing by it. There comes the buckboard. And thanks again. We'll finish burying this man."

"Ain't no sign of it, Mr. Fisher!" someone shouted from the stage.

"You men start searching the wash," he said. Then he walked with Slocum and the others to the buckboard, and assisted the lady into the front seat beside the young man driving.

"I'll send the rest of your luggage on the next stage when it comes by." He checked his gold watch. "It should be here in a short while," he assured them. Tucking away the timepiece, he spoke to the young man. "Harry, have these folks put up in the hotel as my guests and see to their every convenience, please. They'll need new clothing at our expense."

"Oh, yes, sir, Mr. Fisher," the driver said.

"Slocum, thanks, because I am certain your actions and handling of matters saved these folks their lives."

"You're welcome. You do me a favor and you keep an eye on that Crawford. He's dangerous," Slocum said under his breath, and then he climbed in beside Meyers in the back bench. They were off in a lurch, holding to their seats. Slocum looked back. He couldn't see the lawman, but he planned to even the score between them.

7

The stiff new hat thumbed back on his head, Slocum watched Betty as she tried on various outfits. With a bath and shave along with the stiff new clothes, he felt more himself again. He was seated on the wooden chair in the dressmaker's small shop.

"This divided skirt will be good for riding," Betty said, turning for his approval.

"How much riding have you done?" he asked.

"Oh, so you doubt my equestrian skills?" Hands on her hips, she challenged him. The man's broadcloth skirt outlined her firm breasts. Long brown curls spilled down the side of her face and shoulders as she glared at him. The color of her hair was light oak polished until one could almost see one's face in it. He recalled such fine grooming from his youth. Why was what he thought about her appearance so important to her? He was only a hired guard as he saw his place in the matter. What was her husband like? Not much of a man to let his wife traipse around the West looking after business affairs while he hid out in Philadelphia. He'd probably not heard of any damn Apaches back there.

"You don't think I can ride?" She stood in front of him with her hands on her hips.

"I simply asked. I was planning on going to the livery and pick out some horses for us to ride."

"How many?"

"Two to ride is all." He started to rise out of his seat.

"Three. Poor Meyers won't stay in the same town with that bully marshal. He wants to go along."

"Oh, my Gawd. Put him on the next stage for Phoenix. I don't intend to wet-nurse him too."

"Oh, we can't simply abandon the poor man. He has no one."

"I'm not his mother either." It was bad enough for her to want him to wander off in those bronco mountains looking for an old Spanish ranch. Now he had to take that crybaby of a runt along too. He should never have agreed to this crazy search in the first place.

"You won't have to mother him. You'll see, he'll be fine."

"If he falls off his horse, he can walk back. I swear there is not one good reason to have to take him along."

"Have some pity for him." She looked at Slocum, pleading.

"All right, I'll find him a pony."

"I knew you would. He'll be ready to ride at five in the morning."

Slocum reset the new hat on his head and stopped at the door with his back to her. "What if I'd said no?"

"You aren't that bad a person," she said, and hurried across the shop. "Besides, there's a bonus in it for you." When he turned back, her blue eyes met his and he saw the promise in the sparkle.

"Don't overload your wagon, lady," he said privately.

"I won't." Then she winked at him and went off, talking to the seamstress about taking this out and that in.

• • •

"Where's Dirty Shirt Jones these days?" he asked the livery man named Crockett after he concluded renting the three horses and the tack for a week.

"Oh, he was here the other day. Did you know that damn Injun's getting richer by the day?"

"How's that?" Slocum idly chewed on a long straw and listened with his shoulder against the wall.

"Any of them bronco Injuns that run off from the McDowell reservation, they pay him fifty bucks a head for them."

"You mean he captures them?" Slocum pointed the stem at the man.

"No, he just brings their heads back in a tow sack. Business kinda slacked off, though, since he's got so many of them. They're afraid to run off."

"Don't blame them. You see him, tell him Slocum wants to talk to him." He tossed down the straw. A cigar would be better. They sold them over in one of the saloons across the street.

"I sure will, Mr. Slocum. Does he know you?"

"Yeah, we scouted for General Crook a few years ago. I've seen him around since then a time or two."

"How will he find you?" Crockett asked, raising from his rotting wicker chair to cross the room and spit his tobacco out the door.

"No problem. Jones can find whoever he wants."

"Guess that's right." The man wiped his mouth on his dirt-streaked sleeve. "Them horses will be saddled at daylight for you and ready to ride."

"Thanks," Slocum said over his shoulder, and headed for the Red Horse Saloon; he needed a drink and more cigars. Nursemaiding a good-looking married woman all over the Superstitions was one thing, but adding a crybaby like Meyers to it was enough to get drunk over.

"Well, if it ain't the dealer himself. Old Slocum is back in Goldfield, Barney. Ain't he a sight for sore eyes," Milly shouted as she ran over and hugged him, jamming both her big breasts into him and then planting a wet kiss on his mouth.

"It's sure good to see you," she said, leading him to the bar. "Gawdamn, you're all spruced up. Ain't he neat-looking?" she said, her face flushed, her elbows behind her hung on the bar with her full cleavage about to spill out of her dress.

"Stage line bought them for me," he said. "Barney, give me that cigar jar and pour me something good in a glass."

"What about me?" she asked, acting offended.

"Make it a bottle and bring her a glass too."

"We heard you saved some folks in the flood," she said, excited. "What brings you here? I thought you'd come back the next winter, and then the next one." She shrugged her bare shoulders and peered down the front of her red dress as she tugged it up. "But you just forgot us."

"Time got away from me, Milly," he said, raising the glass of whiskey that Barney had poured from the bottle. "Here's to your health."

The liquor was clear and sharp. He agreed to take the bottle, and fished a couple of cigars out of the jar. Then he poured her some whiskey and shoved it over to her.

"Drink up. To the old times!"

"Yeah," she said, hoisting the glass.

He turned and paid Barney for the whiskey and the smokes. Then he followed Milly's ample *derriere* to a table. The place was empty, and he kicked back in a chair to put his boots on the table.

"When did they make that halfwit Crawford the law around here?" he demanded. "He wasn't allowed to carry a gun when he was a night watchman a few years ago."

"You're talking about Marshal Crawford?"

"Yes, he came out where we had the stagecoach wreck and went to pointing a gun around like a madman, accused us of stealing the money and all."

"He's so worthless. No one likes him, but the old marshal got himself killed and no one wanted the job, so the town council hired Crawford." She leaned over with a shake of her head and forced a smile. "Let's talk about you."

"Is he giving you hell?" Slocum asked. There was something in her words, the tone of her voice, that made him ask.

"Let's say he don't know how to treat a lady and damn sure can't treat a whore very nice." She gave a wry shake of her red hair.

"You tell me the truth." He poured another drink and looked her in the eye.

"Hell, when you're in my line of work, you either pay them or treat them. The law—you know what I mean?"

"He beats up women?"

"Yeah, he does."

"I ever catch him, he'll rue the day he did it."

"Be careful, Slocum." She put her hand on his forearm. "He's killed several men since they made him a marshal. All in self-defense, you know what I mean?"

He nodded as he bit the end off the first cigar, spat it on the floor, and then struck a lucifer under the table. He applied the blazing match to the end and then drew in the rich hot smoke. The nicotine slowly was absorbed in his bloodstream and settled him. Jim Crawford would meet his maker if he kept on. Slocum would personally see to that.

8

"What do you mean Harry Johnstone is dead?" Ralph Moore demanded. What was this madman talking about? On top of that, he'd stormed into Moore's office at the bank like someone important. Still, the news Gates brought was much worse than barging into the bank; Moore's stomach fluttered at the thought of the repercussions that could come from the man's death.

"They say they buried him yesterday between Florence Junction and Goldfield," Gates said. "I rode right back here so you would know."

"How did he die?"

"I hear he drowned in a flood that washed the coach away. The driver died too."

"Who else was on that coach?"

"What they told us was that Wells woman, some drummer, and a gambler named Slocum all swam to safety. I guess Johnstone couldn't swim or something."

"Shame that bitch didn't die instead of him." Moore wondered why such a fate had befallen the bank examiner. "I wonder how come he didn't survive. Johnstone, I mean."

"Boss, I have no idea. They were riding up and down that

wash looking for the strongbox when we rode up. No one's found the horses or the driver's body either.''

"Lots of money in that strongbox too," Moore said. "Not the bank's, thank God. It was money being transferred to a bank in San Francisco. They'd still have had their money if they'd kept it here. We've never been robbed. I'll have that story spread around town, show some of those know-it-all mining executives what is the truth. Is she still there in Goldfield?''

"So far as I know. I came right back here. Figured you needed to know about Johnstone's getting killed and all.''

"You did the right thing." Ralph stood at the window and stared out at the small houses that clustered the hills. He needed Johnstone alive. The man had twice covered up some serious shortages in the Pinal National Bank books that could have caused a bank closure and more troubles than that for Moore.

This was the prime reason that he had to have that Iron Mountain mine in operation—to restore the missing funds. He studied the carpeted floor. Why, only two days before he'd taken Johnstone up to the Mexican girl's place. It was an arrangement he had set up with Lola Guarez. She entertained his friends from time to time, and in return he did not foreclose on the young widow. The auditor liked the skinny girl, and she liked him. When he tired of her, usually after twenty-four hours, then the girl's uncle would drive him in a buckboard to the stage stop so Johnstone could go home to his ugly wife and children.

One time Johnstone had shown him a tintype of his wife. She was the ugliest woman Moore had ever seen. Johnstone claimed the picture even flattered her. So it usually took the man twenty-four hours to caper enough around in bed with the Guarez woman, and then he was ready to do banking business elsewhere.

Neither Lola Guarez nor her people would ever talk. But what kind of records regarding the Pinal National Bank did Harry have in his possession? Was there enough information on his bank's business to make Moore regret it if it fell into the wrong hands? He rubbed his smooth-shaven face: the Mexican barber Paulo had sliced him close and put plenty of talc on his cheeks.

"Maybe I need to go to Goldfield and be certain that Harry's records disappear," Moore finally said.

"Are they there?" Bobbie Gates asked.

"Did they say if they found them in the flood?"

Bobbie shook his head. "I don't even know if they found the money yet."

"You and the boys head for Goldfield. I'll meet you behind the hotel. We don't know each other, right?" If those records still existed, they had to be destroyed. If the wrong party got hold of them, it would be all over in Arizona for him.

"Right, meetcha there."

"Well, sir, you'll have to come back again," Moore said in a businesslike voice as he rose and went to open the office door. "Sorry, Mr. Gates, I can't make you a loan on that ranch. You just don't have enough collateral." Ralph held the door open for him to leave.

"I understand, sir," Bobbie said, holding his sombrero before his chest. "I may come back again some day and ask you for another loan."

"Do that, young man, when you get a good nest egg built up. We'll always talk to you."

"Thanks again, Mr. Moore," Bobbie said extra loud, and ducked out through the gate in the low walnut fencing that separated Moore's part of the bank from the teller's portion. Moore watched him exit the bank as he considered his next move. Then he turned as his assistant, Grayson, scoffed, "I would never loan that man money."

"You can never tell when a man like that will have money and we'll need him. A lesson, Grayson. You should never close all avenues. Some may even surprise you. I'm always open to seeing that man. You remember that."

"I always do, and you always tell him no."

"Never mind. I can still do that. Handle things here. I have some business to attend to."

"Someone said they had a stage wreck and a thousand dollars is gone."

"There was one. Spread the word around town that there is safety in putting your money in this bank, understand me?"

"Yes, sir, I will."

Ralph left the bank and took his sorrel from the stable. He did not look forward to the long ride, but this was too important not to handle at once. He would be fortunate not to be drenched on the way by a sudden rainstorm. There had been lots of that this spring; the desert was as green as he could recall. He booted the horse into a long trot.

Slocum had enjoyed enough of Milly's news and the whiskey had settled him. The day shift was over, and several dusty miners came dragging inside, stepping up to the bar and preparing to drink up some of the barrels in stock.

"You leaving?" she asked, looking hurt.

"Yes, I have to get up early and ride out."

"Leaving town already?" She put a hand on his forearm to keep him seated.

"No, but I have an early morning appointment."

"Sounds like business." She wrinkled her nose in disappointment. "Could I entertain you sometime?"

"Yes, you could, my love. Cage yourself a paying one tonight and I'll be by to see you one day soon."

"I'm in the fourth shack up the row. Big number four on the door. You need me for anything, you come by."

"I will," he promised, and kissed her. Then he left the saloon and headed for the hotel. The whiskey had taken the edge off his anger. Inside the hotel, he crossed the lobby and started for the stairs to his room.

"Sooner or later I knew you'd be coming back."

He turned on his heels and mildly surveyed her in the divided black skirt and the man's shirt under the shawl. Betty Wells was certainly all he'd ever imagined her to be under the blue coat.

"Mrs. Wells," he said, touching his hat. "You no doubt are ready to eat supper?"

"I considered I might starve some waiting for you. But you didn't disappoint me, arriving so promptly."

"We didn't—" He couldn't recall whether they had set a date for the meal and he'd had more whiskey than he thought.

"We didn't speak of it, but I expected you," she said, taking his arm and guiding him into the restaurant.

"I may not make the greatest company."

"Why, because you've been drinking?" she asked.

"That and the fact I hate nursemaiding that damn Meyers around the mountains," he said in a loud whisper, really not caring who heard him.

The waiter showed them to a table, and then left them a menu to study. Slocum watched the man retreat across the room. She wasn't listening to a thing he had said about Meyers.

"Mr. Meyers really thinks you are a hero."

"I don't care what he thinks." He turned to look away and try to suppress his aggravation with her.

"My, my, aren't we touchy. What is good to eat here?" Her fresh smile was enough to make his stomach churn.

"The veal here always tasted like paper," he grumbled, picking up the menu again and deciding she was enjoying his discomfort over Meyers.

9

Dawn came, along with a rooster crowing away in the pens behind the stables. The bright spears of sunshine forced everyone to squint when looking to the east. Meyers and Betty were shown their horses. Slocum helped her mount her sorrel. Then, seeing that Meyers would probably circle the yard with his small animal forever trying to get one foot in the stirrup, Slocum stepped in and jerked the gray pony up short. Then he boosted Meyers into the saddle. Heavens, he'd gotten the nearest thing to a kid's pet for the man, and he still couldn't get mounted unassisted. Meyers better not complain, or he could stay at Goldfield.

With the others mounted up, he slid the new Winchester in the boot on his saddle and swung up on the buckskin he'd chosen for himself. At the head of the line, he set his heels to his animal, and they left in a long trot out of town toward the growing sun. Before the day was out he wanted to cover plenty of country. He had packed some things in a poke for them to eat for lunch, and canteens were tied on each saddle.

This ranch of Betty's was somewhere beyond Weaver's Needle, and that was a half day's ride if they sidled along. Besides, at the first sign of Indians they were turning back.

That was, if they were lucky enough to cut any sign before the savages found them. He did not intend to stay in the mountains at night and get their throats cut, so he'd taken no bedrolls. They could headquarter in Goldfield, see all the possible sites, and get back by dark each evening. The days at this time of year were a good twelve hours long anyway.

"Keep out of the cholla." He pointed to the spiny jointed cactus on the slope. "That will cripple a horse and you can't get out of it once you get in it. Stay away from it," he said loud enough so both of them could hear him.

He glanced back at the stiff-looking Meyers bringing up the rear. Perhaps one day in the saddle would take care of the drummer. If he became sore enough, twelve hours in the saddle would cure Meyers of this foolishness of having to go along with them. Slocum had no intention of letting the man slow down their searching—whatever happened to him.

Slocum halted them after they were several miles deep in the range, and told them to dismount and let their horses blow at the foot of a mountain grade. For the lady's benefit, he pointed to a large house-sized rock that could shield her business, and nodded with his head to Meyers to take off into the mesquite on the flat along the dry wash.

"Is it safe?" Meyers asked, looking around suspiciously.

"So far," he said, and tied the horses up so he could do the same thing.

He still didn't know a thing about Betty's husband or how she'd ended up with this land grant. In fact, he had mentally appraised the situation several times, and all he could patch together about her was what she had said beside the fire in his brief taste of passion with her—"I'm married."

Back at the horses, they drank from canteens and remounted. Meyers made it up by himself, and Slocum looked to the sky, grateful for some providential help. He led the way up the narrow trail.

"This path looks well used," she said behind him.

"Yes, the Army patrols this about every week. They ride over it a lot. The Apaches must use it too."

"Oh," Meyers said, looking around as they climbed the steep switchback and went on upward.

"There ain't no Apaches been here today," Slocum said, satisfied nothing but shod horses had used the trail in recent times.

On top of the windy high point, the tall shaft of gray rock called Weaver's Needle stood out by itself, towering over the rest of the jumbled red, ocher, and gray ranges.

"They named that for a mountain man, Paul Weaver," he said. He booted the buckskin downgrade anxious to get out of the sharp wind. "You ever get lost up here, you can always find your way out by coming to that Needle. Most of the main trails fork around it."

"Did you hear him, Mr. Meyers?"

"Yes, I did, but Mrs. Wells, I don't intend to lose his shirt-tail," the small man said, pushing his spectacles back up his nose.

Slocum was proud of their progress. He'd left the main trail that he had taken once before going to Picket Post to talk with Alex Baird about their claim. On the return trip, he had ridden back to Goldfield with a troop of soldiers from Ft McDowell, so he felt confident in his knowledge of that area. From the base of the Needle east, of course, he was in unknown land, but few white folks went in or out and lived to talk about it. He also was basing his decision to go into this portion of the mountains on the fact that most of the Apaches were on reservations.

"There is grass here," she said, riding at his stirrup along a small stream of water.

"It is a very wet spring. That stream normally would be dry."

"How do you know that?"

"No moss on the bottom of the bed. In year-round water, it grows moss."

"Are you a stock man?" she asked.

"I've herded some. This is cow country. Too much cactus and sharp spines would tear the wool off sheep."

"What kind of cattle?"

"Tough ones. Texas longhorn cows and good sure-footed bulls. You might get some Scottish shorthorns to cross on them."

"Have you ever been a ranch foreman?"

He shook his head, and studied the high cliffs that rose like organ pipes for any sign of a threat. The sloping talus rock bases could also shelter an Indian. On edge about the reputation of these canyons, he knew this was no place to simply shuffle through.

"There's a corral!" she said, excited.

"Hold up," he said, seeing ahead the poles and posts of a large pen in the narrow valley. It certainly had been a large undertaking for such a place, and it looked in good repair. He reached under his leg and removed the Winchester. Into the chamber he levered a brass cartridge, and signaled for them to stay there.

Whoever had built such a structure in these mountains? He advanced through the lacy mesquites until he finally could appraise the entire pen. Beyond the corral stood a small adobe house without windows, the door fallen to the ground. Was this Betty's ranch? Certainly someone had used this as some sort of staging place. He dismounted and dropped the reins. The gelding was enough cow pony to stay ground-tied.

His mouth dry, he advanced on the shack. He checked the ground for tracks, but only a pack rat and some small birds had been there since the rains. Still, he searched for the telltale scuff of a moccasin. Halting short of the porch, the rifle in his sweaty hands, he tried to see inside the building. No use. He stepped up and drove through the door, the hammer cocked.

A desert rodent scurried for cover, but as his eyes became accustomed to the darker room, he could see it was empty save for some broken handmade furniture and smashed pottery left by past inhabitants.

"It's all right. Come on in," he said with a wave to the others from the doorway.

"Do you think this is part of the ranch?" she asked, dismounting, as he shoved the Winchester back in the scabbard. From the corner of his eye, he saw the drummer scurry around behind the adobe corner to perform some needed body function.

"Did anyone ever describe the ranch headquarters to you?" he asked, arching and stretching his stiff back.

"Yes, and he said the main house was tile-roofed and very fancy." She had disappointment written on her face as she peered inside the adobe hovel.

"I see no signs of that ever being here. He might have lied to you."

"No, he had been an employee of the family. He had lived and worked on this ranch. I spoke to him in Mexico."

"He had been here?"

"Yes, worked here for many years."

"Why didn't you get him to bring you?" he asked.

"He was blind and too old."

"Indians!" Meyers's chilling scream caused both of them to blink at each other. His rifle in his hand, Slocum raced back to defend their horses, unable to see the terrified-sounding man or the Indians behind the building.

Then the source of all of the man's screams came into view riding a big Roman-nosed gray horse. The Yuma-Apache, well over six feet, wore an amused grin when he spotted Slocum.

"Dirty Shirt Jones," Slocum called out to the man under the unblocked gray hat.

"You know him?" she asked with her voice catching in her throat.

"I sent for him. They tell me you're making big money," Slocum said, approaching the man.

"Got three in here," he said, patting the bulging hundred-pound flour sack.

"You ever been to the ranch headquarters of the Spanish grant?"

"A long time ago. It is a place of the dead." He shook his heavy head in disgust.

"I know what you speak of," Slocum said, knowing that Apaches disliked places where people had died. "But where is it?"

"It is beyond Iron Mountain." Jones shifted his big frame to turn in the saddle, and despite his grey horse's size, it was forced by the man's move to resituate his feet. Then he pointed to the east. "It is maybe a day's ride from here."

"If we don't find it today, when will you be back to Gold-field?"

"In the morning."

"Good," he said, noticing Meyers was keeping to the shade of the porch. "We'll meet you at the livery in the morning and you can show Mrs. Wells here her ranch."

Jones nodded he had heard. Then he leaned over and spoke under his breath to Slocum. "That little guy over there, he ain't very brave, is he?"

Slocum shook his head.

"Mr. Jones, is the ranch house still standing there?" Betty asked. "The one with the tile roof and all?"

He nodded in reply, and then reined the gray around and with a wave left them. In a trot, he rode off down their back trail toward Goldfield.

"See? He knows there is a ranch house. What did he have in the sack?" she asked, acting excited as she stood beside Slocum.

"The heads of three renegades."

"Oh!" she said, paling at the notion and turning away with a look of distaste.

"What's the matter?" Meyers asked, joining them.

"She wondered what was in that sack on Dirty Shirt Jones' saddle."

"What was it?"

"The decapitated heads of three renegade Indians. He's riding to Fort McDowell to collect the bounty on them."

The drummer rushed around the building and out of view; Slocum could hear him retching. He looked back at the Needle sticking up from the mountains and shook his head—there were worse things than decapitated heads. He could recall two or three times he had seen the aftermath of Apache torture, people whose brains had been boiled over a slow fire before they'd expired. He tried to shake the visions of the victims as he told both of them to mount up—they had a ways further to go before they needed to turn back.

10

"What do you mean they rode out?" Ralph demanded as he faced Gates in the alley behind the hotel. The noon sun shone high overhead as the two men stood out of sight of the main street.

"I know this much," his henchman said. "They rented some horses down at the livery and rode out at dawn. The gambler, the drummer, and her, and they rode off up into the Superstitions."

"They won't find shit." Moore dismissed their efforts. How could such a combination find a thing in those jumbled mountains? "Why did she get a gambler and a drummer for guides? The damn renegades will kill them and we won't have to."

"I ain't so sure. They say this gambler was around here about two years ago, and he might know more than we think about Injuns and the Superstitions."

"What's his name?"

"Slocum."

"Never heard of him. He's just some smooth talker. But why take the drummer along? For a bodyguard?" He became so amused at the notion that he had to put his hand on the clapboard siding of the hotel to support himself while he laughed at the absurd arrangement the stupid woman had made. Still, he couldn't forget her ripe body and his own inability to work her into a compromising position.

"That stuff you want is in the stage office," Gates said in a low voice. "I heard them say they found Johnstone's stuff and are going to ship it tomorrow to Prescott."

"Good, then we've got to get it tonight, Bobbie," he said, recovering his composure. "You be certain that marshal is occupied. And we'll get that luggage out of there and no one will be the wiser."

"What'll we do about the stage agent on duty?" Gates hissed.

"If there is one, we'll bump him over the head. He won't see us."

"Yeah, and we sure need to take care of Crawford beforehand. He's a madman."

"Does he drink?"

"Some, but he likes whores. Maybe I can get one of those row girls to entertain him while we're robbing the office."

"They'd spill the beans on you." Moore shook his head. He didn't need some bitch rattling away about who'd hired her to distract the deputy. Whores couldn't take much slapping around and they'd talk. Crawford would figure that out even if he were an idiot.

"Yeah. *I* know. I'll get someone to send him out to the wreck around dark. No way he can be back here before morning." Gates beamed.

"Who will do that? He'll know you and your boys did it."

"Damn, that's right. This sure is taking lots of thinking, ain't it, Boss." Gates put his back to hotel wall, jammed his hands in his pants, and studied his boot toes.

Then Moore had an idea. "What if you start a rumor around town that the strongbox broke and there is money up and down that wash. That would cause a big rush and he'd have to go down there to protect the stage line's interest.''

"What's going to make them believe that?'' Gates blinked against the noon sun when he looked up.

"This money,'' Ralph said as he counted out fifteen one-dollar bills from his wallet. "You go make this money as muddy as you can, then you dry it, and tonight that is going to prove you found it in the wash as part of the loot when you spend it openly in the saloon.''

"Yeah. I see why you're a banker and I'm just a helper. Mr. Moore, that is the smartest thing I ever heard of.''

"Just so you make it work,'' Moore reminded him. If Bobbie could do that convincingly enough, it would cause a stampede for the wash and they would have the entire town to themselves. Once those Johnstone papers were destroyed, then they could leisurely get rid of that woman and those two clods riding with her. And he could get on with taking over the Iron Mountain mine. He was so pleased with his idea that he figured he might as well find himself a sporting woman to while away the afternoon with. What was that redhead's name?

11

The April afternoon wind tore at them as they rode along the narrow hogback. Slocum was forced to hold his head to the side to keep his new hat on. The buckskin led the way down the narrow gravel trail. Slocum looked at the pines across the way on the top of the far mountains to the south. They capped an entire range almost due south.

"What are you looking at, Slocum?" Betty asked, riding up beside him.

"Those pines. I'd seen a few scattered around, but that mesa's covered with them." No one had ever mentioned them before, but he wanted to see them up close.

"How far away are they?"

"Too far to ride today." He looked back at Meyers, sitting slumped in the saddle, holding his hat wadded up in one hand to save it being blown away, his face red from the day's sun.

"We're going back," he shouted to the man.

Meyers nodded woodenly.

"When we come back with this Jones, can we camp up here and get further back?" she asked.

"We can. It's your money. It'll cost you for gear, grub, and a packhorse or mule. Maybe close to forty bucks."

"I can afford it. What will Jones charge to lead us to the ranch?"

"A couple bucks a day. He makes big wages getting renegades only because no one else can find them up here but him."

"He'll be worth that. Slocum, you know about cattle. Can they sustain themselves on this grass?"

"They should, but not too many. This is a very wet season and there's lots of six-weeks grass coming up. Yes, you can run cows up here, but you will need some vaqueros from Mexico who aren't afraid of rocks and cactus."

"Can you find such men for me?"

"Sure," he said, and drew in deep through his nostrils. He would do about anything for a pretty woman, even a married one. He set spurs to the buckskin and took the lead going back. It had been a day wasted roaming around, but they'd have Jones to help them from then on.

Where was that scoundrel Alex Baird? Slocum gazed across the towering purple cliffs and the red-gray caps of mountains rising like plowed furrows to the distant Four Peaks. Some day he would find him.

They reached Goldfield after the sun had set. Wearily they dropped from their saddles. Even Slocum held onto the horn until his legs were strong enough to hold his weight. There was a ranch up there, and nothing would sway Betty now that she had heard from Jones that there were buildings.

"Grain them, and we'll also need a packhorse tomorrow," Slocum told Crockett.

"I've got a good one," he said as they stripped off the saddles. Then Meyers and Betty carried theirs inside, leaving Slocum with the man.

"You see Jones today?" Crockett asked, leading the three horses back toward the pens.

"Yes."

"I've got a note here for you from Milly," the man said under his breath. "She said to keep it secret."

"Thanks." Slocum said, taking it from him. He stuck it in his coat pocket and strode over to Mrs. Wells, who had come from the tack room. "We'll need to get bedrolls, supplies, and food."

"Will you help me pick it all out?" she asked.

"Certainly."

"Mr. Meyers, are you going with us?" she asked, turning to the drummer. "We're going to get supplies for tomorrow."

"Sure," the shorter man said, wincing as he started to walk out of the livery office. The drummer walked so bow-legged Slocum wanted to laugh at him. How much more could the little man take? The long day had taken a toll on him, no doubt. Still, he acted enthused about going along with them to the mercantile, maybe just to stay in their protective company while Crawford was nearby.

"You sore?" Slocum asked.

"Worse than that," he muttered with his hands on his hips.

"We're going out at dawn again."

"I'll be there," Meyers said.

Slocum nodded that he'd heard the man's intentions, and hurried to walk beside Mrs. Wells. They strode up the street as the sounds of a tinny piano carried into the street. It was the music he knew came from the Kid's fingers in the Gold Dust Saloon. A skinny man, the Kid looked hardly older than a boy, and played the keys with such skill that many tough men stood around and cried recalling the music of their past.

Inside the mercantile, she let Slocum order what they needed for camping out. Then she stepped forward when he finished and drew the money out of her small purse.

"You got a gun?" Slocum asked Meyers with an elbow to stir the man.

"No." The drummer looked shocked at the notion.

"Buy one while we're here and I'll show you how to shoot it." Slocum then told the young clerk, "Get him that small .30-caliber Colt in the case, a holster, and a box of shells."

"I never—" But Meyers stepped in and paid for the revolver. Then he buckled on the holster warily and slapped the empty revolver in it.

"You don't need to load it yet," Slocum assured him, then turned to the clerk behind the counter. "Young man, we'll need this order at first light to pack on a horse."

"I'll be here to do that," the flush-faced clerk said.

"Good."

"If we have all we need, I am famished," Betty said, pushing her hair back from her face with the back of her hand. "Gentlemen, let's go eat."

"Yes, ma'am," Slocum agreed. He was ready to feast on something. They strode the boardwalk toward the hotel. Meyers adjusted his empty gun a half-dozen times walking to the restaurant.

"I'll be right in, you two find a table," Slocum said, recalling the note in his pocket. He paused for a minute under the lamplight on the hotel porch and unfolded the page, which smelled of perfume.

Slocum
Watch out for a banker in town called Ralph Moore from
Picket Post. He could mean big trouble. He asked lots of
questions about you today.
Milly

Moore? He stepped inside the lobby. Where had he heard that name before? Of course. From Mrs. Wells. Yes, she'd had a run in with him too. Slocum looked at the wagon-wheel lamp overhead. What was Moore's part in this matter? He would need to learn more about the man. Bless Milly's heart for the warning—he owed the lady for it. Pocketing the paper, he hurried off to join them in the restaurant.

12

From the poker game at the side table, through the haze of smoke of the Five Star Saloon, Ralph could see Gates and two of his men come in the swinging door. They sauntered up to the bar, and he was so satisfied that they could pull off what they'd agreed on, he looked down at his hand.

"You in or out, mister?" the bearded miner asked him from across the table.

"Let me see," Ralph said, and carefully fanned his cards out. "I'll cover that bet of yours."

"Boys," Gates said loud enough everyone could hear. "We found enough dirty money down in the Saguaro Wash tonight to start us a bank.

"Yes, sir, plumb shame," he continued. "We didn't have enough light. It got dark on us, but we're going back in the morning. Why, there's enough dirty money in that wash to start a new bank in this town. Couldn't believe it myself."

"Let's see that money," someone demanded as they crowded in around him to examine the soiled dollars.

"Muddy enough," someone else said by the bar. Gates was drawing a crowd as Ralph put down three queens and two kings, then drew a fresh Havana cigar from his silk vest pocket.

"Can you beat that?" Moore pointedly asked the miner.

"Why, hell, no."

There was more clamoring about Gates's "find" in the wash and the lost shipment from Picket Post than was mentioned out loud. Could it be he had found the money? It took the majority of the customers less than ten minutes to decide that that was in fact what had happened. Excited men began to rush out the front doors for home to get their gear or horses to ride. Soon, the saloon was empty, except for the players at the table and Gates and his boys. Three of the cardplayers, obviously captivated by Gates's story, then excused themselves and left, leaving only Ralph and two others.

He rifled the cards in a quick shuffle. The two men, the miner and a gambler calling himself Clanton, acted as if they wanted to win back their losses to Ralph. In the corner of his vision he saw the marshal come inside, look around, and rush to the bar.

"Let me see that money you're passing around here," he demanded.

"What's wrong, Marshal? It's only muddy—"

"I said give the damn stuff to me." Then Crawford swiped the money from Gates's hand and looked at it under the light.

"What are you doing?" Gates complained.

"This here is evidence." Crawford waved it in the man's face. "You found it in Saguaro Wash?"

"Yeah, lying in the mud."

"Then I say this is express company money lost in the stage wreck."

"How in the hell can you prove that! It ain't got their name on it!" Gates shouted.

"You want to be locked up? Coming in here and causing a damn rush down there? Now I'll have to go and get back

all that money they find. I ought to lock you up for causing . . .''

"Causing what?"

"I'll think of a charge. Now empty your pockets. I want all
this money."

"Gentlemen?" Ralph asked, poised to deal the next hand
and satisfied the lawman was about to leave town. Yes, his
trick was working as planned.

"Deal me out," Clanton said, and then lowered his voice.
"How in the hell can he take that money from that cowboy
up there?"

"Search me," Ralph said under his breath. "But by damn
he did it. He's the law."

"By Gawd, if he tried to take that money from me, I'd shoot
him."

"Yes, I agree."

"You going looking for any of the money?" Clanton asked.

"Probably will, come first light," Ralph said as if mildly
interested. He needed to get back to his bank and the wash
was en route, so he wasn't lying to the man. His prime concern
was getting possession of Johnstone's papers. Then Gates and
the gang could figure out how to get rid of this Slocum and
the woman. They could make it look like Indians did it.

Strange how hesitant Milly had been speaking about the
man. Almost like that buxom bitch had something to hide. He
hadn't even considered the notion at the time, but the longer
he thought about her answers, the more convinced he was she
was covering up something. A little slapping around and she'd
talk. He'd do that before he left town. Then he'd have the
answers.

"I got to get up and work tomorrow if there's anyone in
town left to work," the miner said, looking around the empty
barroom. "Damn bunch of fools jump up and run off at any
rumor."

"Everyone wants to get rich," Ralph said. The miner agreed.

Crawford had left the saloon with Gates following him, protesting over his seizure of the muddy dollars. The plan had worked perfectly in Ralph's book; all they needed now was a successful burglary of the stage office. In order to divert suspicion, though, they needed to take more than Johnstone's things out of the office. Ralph sat back and smoked his cigar and drank the bonded whiskey, until he finally excused himself to the glass-polishing barkeep.

"Slow night," he said as he rose and then tossed the man a silver cartwheel for a tip.

"Thank you, sir," the man said. "Yes, that money even tempted me to close up and be there at first light."

"How much is out there?" Ralph asked as if he'd never heard of the matter.

"Ten thousand, I heard."

"My, my, that is a lot of money," he said, knowing full well the amount was one thousand. All the more lure for the treasure hunt. He went outside, searched around, and then slipped into the alley when he saw no one or nothing.

"Crawford rode out an hour ago," Gates hissed from the shadows.

"Good. How does it look?"

"Looks too easy. One clerk inside. He's busy with invoices. We hit him over the head and take what we want."

"Be careful. I'll meet you on the road in the morning. You will need to get up there at the wash and act like you're looking for the rest of the money. Oh, yes, and while you're in the stage office, take more than Johnstone's things so they don't point a finger at us." He meant himself, but Bobbie didn't need to hear it that way.

"We can handle it."

"Good," he said, and turned on his heels. In a few minutes,

he was back at his dark hotel room where he could observe the stage office from the second story. He stood by the window and watched.

Some shadows began to move around inside the office, and then the clatter of horse hooves came from down the alley as he undid his necktie. With that task completed, he could ride home in the morning after he visited the whore again and learned all that she really knew about this Slocum. He rubbed his lower lip with the side of his hand as he considered her—she'd learn never to lie to him.

Sunup formed a gray line on the horizon. Slocum hurried about on foot, leading the packhorse across the street to the mercantile. He and the clerk loaded the supplies into the panniers that hung on the packsaddle, and then they tied the bedrolls on top. Betty came over on horseback, leading his buckskin horse. Meyers pushed his glasses up to the bridge of his nose as he rode up with some authority on his pony.

"Where's Jones?" she asked, searching around the street for a sign of the man.

"He'll be along. Don't worry, Indians aren't on our time. Jones says he's coming, count on it."

"How can we ride to the ranch headquarters if we don't know the way?"

"We head up there and Jones will show up. He always does. He probably is cashing in those heads this morning, and that's what's keeping him."

"I wish you'd never mentioned that," she said, turning away with a distasteful look. "Oh, the livery man said someone robbed the stage office last night and that Marshal Crawford is gone with most of the men. Something about someone finding the strongbox contents in the wash."

"What did they steal from the office?" Slocum glanced down the street.

"I don't know. He just said there was a robbery."

Slocum checked the cinch and then jerked down the stirrup and climbed aboard. Why rob a stage office? Couldn't be much cash in it. Someone had to be desperate for money.

"I wonder if they stole my sample cases," Meyers asked out loud. "I left them there rather than haul them upstairs to the hotel room."

"They got some soap if they did." Slocum laughed and took the lead of the packhorse. "You don't need them anymore, do you?"

"No, sir, that's why I left them there," Meyers said, booting his mount forward with newfound enthusiasm. "I'm through working for the Bailey Soap Company."

"What do you plan to do?" she asked, riding abreast with them.

"Maybe—well, Mrs. Wells, I'm not certain, but I am enjoying the outdoors and even riding, though I must say I am sore."

Wait until tonight, Slocum thought to himself as they trotted out of Goldfield for the mountains. The sun's first light was shining on top of the high wall of the Superstitions on their right.

Ralph stood in the hotel room window blinking his gritty eyes. That damn Wells woman was down there in the street on horseback. He recognized her even in the dim light. The drummer must be the one wearing the bowler and riding the short horse. The man under the felt hat and on the buckskin had to be Slocum. He could see this man was no ordinary gambler; he rode like a vaquero, with the easy step-up of a man hard as rock. Perhaps he had misjudged his opposition.

He would learn all about him from Milly. She'd have lots to tell him before he was through with her. He began to dress, his mind making plans for how he would draw the information from her.

In less than ten minutes, he was at the number-four shack and rapping on the door. Hoping she had no overnight customer staying, he waited as her sleep-choked voice said, "Hold your damn horses, I'm coming."

The door barely parted, and he shoved his weight into it and spilled her backwards. In an instant, he was standing before her and drove a doubled fist into her belly. She bent over and choked for her breath as he closed the door, then turned to face her in the dimly lit room.

"What the hell's wrong with you?" she gasped.

He jerked her upright by her curly hair and with his face close to hers, demanded answers.

"What answers?"

"Who is this Slocum?"

"A gambler, like I told you," she said, rising to the pain of his hair-pulling. She was naked under the thin duster, and her large breasts shook as he lifted her to her toes.

"You're hurting me. Stop! I know nothing."

"No, that ain't all. You know more," he said through his teeth.

"I swear—you're hurting me."

He slapped her face so hard his palm stung. She'd either get smarter or get beaten up. She wasn't that tough; she'd talk.

"I don't know what you want," she sobbed.

"I want everything you know about him."

"He was only here—" Her words were cut off by his back-hand to her cheek that popped her head sideways.

"Tell me what you know about him!"

"He's wanted by the law," she finally said. Tears streamed down her face. She tried to grasp his hand and bring down his fist wrapped in her hair, but he jerked it so hard she quit.

"Where is he wanted at?"

"Kansas, I think they said."

"What's his full name?" He pulled her close to his face.

"You're hurting me."

"Tell me his real full name."

"John Slocum is all I know—I swear that's what those two bounty hunters called him that came here looking for him."

He shoved her roughly onto the bed. Slocum was wanted. He could learn all about that from the law in Kansas. But this matter wasn't over. He looked down at her as she cried and protectively held the side of her head where he had pulled her curls. There was no way that he could trust her. First, he undid his pants. He needed to use her. Then he could decide what he must do to silence her.

With rough hands, he spread her knees apart and climbed between them. He thrust himself inside her and glared down as she sobbed and moaned about how much he had hurt her. Deaf to her complaining, he continued to plow deeper and deeper. Hurt her? Why, he'd show her hurt. He pinched her great breasts and then grinned at her cries of distress. Finally he came in a last drive. Looking at her in disgust, he withdrew himself and straightened as she twisted away. Her fleshy shoulders were shaking as she cried on the pillow.

He used the edge of the undone bedsheet to wipe away the slick traces of her from his manhood. Considering what he must do to stop her from talking to anyone, he drew up his pants from around his ankles. A search in his pocket produced a large jackknife with a keen edge. He studied her bare form, face-down, sobbing. Then, his mind set on his next action, he opened the knife. Methodically, he crawled upon the edge of the bed. Next, he jammed his knee down hard in the center of her back to hold her belly-down on the mattress. In a flash, he jerked her head back with a handful of curls, and quick as a cat cut off her screaming with the razor edge of his blade applied to her throat.

No witnesses allowed.

13

They rested their horses at a noon stopover deep in the Superstitions past Weaver's Needle. Stale canteen water and hard beef jerky made their lunch. Betty and Meyers acted content to be out of the saddle. Slocum left them and climbed to a high point overlooking the jumbled land. On his belly, he used an Army-issue brass telescope to search for any sign of Apaches.

He sprawled on the sun-warm flat rock and scanned the mountains around them. Years of scouting told him what to search for. A horse or even a colorful piece of cloth impaled on a cactus could be a sign of their presence.

"Find anything?" she asked, crawling in beside him.

"Nothing so far," he said, glancing over at her as she stretched out and rested on her elbows.

"What do you know about this banker Moore?" he asked, scanning the visible slopes around them.

"He is a very mean man." She looked away from him. "In his office, he threatened me if I didn't sell him my claim. Then when I didn't, he really grew angry. I thought he was going to strike me, and if we hadn't been in the bank, I think he would have. I do carry a small derringer, and that night, uninvited, he came to my hotel room and, had I not had the gun, I believe he would have forced himself upon me.''

"You had to run him off with a gun?'' He shook his head in disbelief—what kind of person was this Moore?

"Yes, I did, and then I hurried and left Picket Post. You know the rest of my story. Why are you asking?''

"Have you seen this Moore in Goldfield?''

"No, why? Is he there?'' Her violet eyes widened in disbelief.

"Yes. According to a friend of mine, he showed up asking lots of questions about me.''

"I'm sorry I have brought you into my troubles.'' She kept staring ahead. The tip of her tongue wet her lips as she shook her head in disapproval.

"No worry about that,'' Slocum said, "but I like to know my enemies. What's his interest in the land grant?''

"I don't know, but he obviously wants my title.''

"Damn strange why any banker wants a ranch that is so overrun with Apaches you couldn't make a dime with it. There has to be another reason that he wants your deed. It is a key to something.'' He pushed up on his hands and knees. "We better ride on.''

"Your friend Jones isn't here yet. Suppose something happened to him.''

"Jones will be along. He said he would.'' Slocum reached down and pulled her to her feet. Again he met her violet blue eyes for a long second and felt a tingle in his senses. The scout was coming. He was more concerned about what this Moore was up to. And her—she was too much woman to run around all over alone.

Late afternoon shadows were cast over them as they rode single-file down a deep narrow canyon; they spooked a small herd of javelina. The small pigs scurried from a large bed of pancake cactus and clattered off down the canyon. Their retreating grunts and squeals were loud in the confines of the mountains. Slocum reined up with a grin, and then twisted in the saddle to look back and reassure her and Meyers, who led the packhorse.

"Nothing, but some javelinas," he said, and turned back, prepared to ride on. "They're little wild pigs that live in these mountains."

"What were they doing?" she asked.

"Eating prickly pear cactus," he said.

"Oh, they weren't," she said, dismissing him.

"Look over there at the ones they've chewed up." He pointed to the torn-up pads where they had grazed.

"How do their stomachs take the spines?"

"Made of iron, I guess." He booted the buckskin on.

"I heard they would attack people," Meyers said from the rear.

"They might," Slocum agreed as he caught sight of running water ahead in the small wash they followed. "But they always run from me. We'll make camp ahead. We need to get a fire going before dark."

He studied the talus rock slopes that rose into the pink and yellow sheer cliffs above them. No sign of an Apache. So far they'd been lucky. How close could they be to the ranch? They were several hours' ride past the corrals they'd found the day before. He would be glad when Jones arrived.

They dismounted on a grassy flat and unsaddled. He put the saddle horses on leads, afraid hobbles might not be enough. Then he let Betty lead them down to the stream for a drink while he and Meyers unloaded the packhorse.

"Why is she so set on seeing this ranch anyway?" Meyers asked in a soft voice, taking the bedrolls and stacking them.

"Beats me," Slocum said, watching her stand down by the stream and hold the lines as the horses drank deeply of the small stream.

"Not only is it dangerous, but she can't stay up here. You know that."

"Maybe her husband will come up and live with her."

"Funny thing about that too." Meyers shook his head in disapproval.

"What's that?" Slocum asked, hoisting the pannier box off the horse.

"Where in the heck is he?" Meyers whispered with a frown on his face.

"Damned if I know," Slocum said, walking around to the other side and lifting the other loaded pannier off the horse with a great effort. Finding a place, he set it beside the other one and straightened.

"I'll water him," Meyers said with a shrug, and led the packhorse away.

Slocum agreed, and went to gathering fuel. They helped him collect more, and soon he had a small fire going, but one hot enough to boil the coffee and roil the dry brown beans around. The rich wood smoke in his nose, he squatted on his boot heels and tended the food and fire. Finally satisfied the coffee was made, he called them in and poured them each a cup.

"No Jones yet," she reminded him over the lip of her cup.

"He'll come along," he reassured her. His eyes narrowed to slits as he studied the golden light on top of the mountain to the west. It soon would be sundown, but Jones would come.

"What about my gun?" Meyers asked.

Slocum took the man's pistol and showed him how the single-action cocked and fired. He had the man point the pistol and repeatedly pull the trigger with an empty cylinder. The hammer fell over and over as he told Meyers to simply point the gun. Shots at close range were never aimed—point and shoot.

"I think I see," the man said as Slocum loaded the Colt

and then unloaded it, making the drummer do it repeatedly until he was satisfied he knew the principles.

"Remember, point and fire," Slocum said, stirring the beans.

"I will."

"No bullet in the chamber under the hammer. It might go off and shoot you in the leg."

"Five shells are all I need in the pistol?"

"Right. Just don't shoot me in the back."

"Oh, I won't."

When Slocum turned back to his beans, he saw her approving nod. Seated on the ground, her legs tucked under her, she obviously appreciated his teaching the man about the revolver.

"Beans be done in an hour," Slocum promised, and took up the pot to pour some more coffee around. "I hate to break my teeth on beans, don't you?"

"Yes," she said with a smile, and held out her cup for more coffee.

"Someone's coming," Meyers announced, and unholstered his six-gun.

"Don't shoot. I can tell by the horse's gait it's Dirty Shirt Jones."

"How can you do that?"

"He rides a pacer and there ain't many of them, especially in the Superstitions."

Jones trotted up in the twilight, watered his gray horse in the stream, and then remounted and rode up on the flat. His horse was winded and lathered from the hard ride.

Slocum introduced him to the other two again, and then asked the scout how much further they must go.

"We can be there in the morning," Jones said, and then looked around at the three of them before he dipped out a plate of beans from the pot for himself. He sat down on the ground and accepted a cup of coffee from Slocum.

"You been busy?" Slocum asked.

"Sumbitches, new lieutenant at McDowell." The scout shook his head. "They only pay me for one."

"You had three."

"New man at McDowell. Plenty cheap. He thinks Army can find them. So I'm going to let him find them bronco sumbitches. Old Nan Tan Lupan come by, Jones talk to him about this cheap lieutenant."

"Who's he going to talk to?" Betty asked.

"General George Crook—Apaches call him the Gray Wolf," Jones said for their benefit.

"Oh," she said, sounding impressed. "You say we can ride to the ranch in a few hours from here?"

"Easy," Jones said, and busied himself spooning in beans.

She rose and walked to where the horses grazed. Slocum wondered what was wrong, and followed her.

"Something the matter?" he asked.

"Yes," she sniffled with her back to him. "I've waited since I was a little girl for this to happen. And tomorrow . . ." She blotted her eyes on a kerchief. "And tomorrow I am finally going to see it."

"Don't expect too much. I'm certain there have been lots of Indian raids made on the ranch." He didn't want her as disappointed as he expected her to be when they finally arrived there.

"I won't." She walked into his arms and buried her face in his shoulder. "You knew Jones would come and kept telling me. I just couldn't see how this would ever work out. I have worked so hard and so long for this—I just knew that I was in another dead end."

He raised her chin up and looked into her wet eyes, which sparkled under the tears in the starlight. She turned her head and he kissed her. He closed his eyes to the facts and enjoyed her hungry mouth until they finally stood apart, out of breath and shaken.

"Damn," he swore with a head shake, and started to turn.

"Thank you," she said softly after him, and he went back to camp.

14

"There ain't no money here," a disgusted man said with a long-handle shovel on his shoulder as he climbed out of the wash. His boots and the legs of his pants were caked with white and red mud.

Ralph pushed his sorrel alongside the gulch. Others too were giving up and staggering out, weary from a lack of sleep and the disappointment. Many carried lamps they'd brought to see in the night. He saw no sign of Gates or any of the gang members. They should be somewhere—he had told him to be close by. Anger began to rise in his chest the further he rode. Where were they at?

Did they want the damn law suspicious? He booted the sorrel on, passing several more mumbling returnees coming out of the wash. If they ever learned this whole thing had been a hoax, the perpetrators might be sentenced to hang at a miners' court. Then he saw several riderless horses ahead on a flat and Crawford standing among a throng of men. He pushed his sorrel ahead to see what was happening.

"Crawford, that money is ours!" an angry man shouted.

"No, it isn't, boys. You're obstructing justice!"

"No," someone shouted. "We're going to obstruct *you*."

He could see by then that during the night's rush, someone had unearthed the strongbox and Crawford now had his foot on it. Good. The ploy had worked, and no one would even suspect a thing since they'd found the real box. A shame that Gates didn't find it. That was the smart-ass mine owners' money. They were transferring it to San Francisco rather than deposit it in his bank. There should be a way—the notion of not being able to get it for his own purposes made him sick to his stomach—but he couldn't do much about the matter.

Crawford finally barged through the crowd of men and tied the box to his saddle horn; then he rode off for Goldfield. The rest of the men groveled among themselves like kicked dogs.

"We got everything," Gates said under his breath as he stopped beside Ralph's stirrup.

"Good. Now go back and kill that woman and the drummer."

"What about Slocum?"

"Him too if you can. If not, we can give him to the law."

"Is he wanted?"

"Yes, but kill him too if you can."

"We'll do it."

"They took a packhorse into the Superstitions this morning with them."

"No problem. Consider it done. I'll save those papers we got for you till we get back to the ranch?" Gates asked.

"Yes." Ralph booted his horse away. They needed no more public contact with each other. Just so they did what they had to. He should have killed the Wells woman earlier like he did that redheaded whore, and then this whole business would all be over.

Slocum built a fire in the dark to cook their breakfast over. Betty squatted close by under a blanket, and shivered against the predawn cold of the canyon as she watched him.

"How long have you been working on getting this ranch?" he asked.

"Forever. My father did geology work for the DeVaga family. He was a guest at the ranch house twenty years ago. He did business with the family in Mexico, and then came up here and visited the ranch with the Don. He even made sketches of the place and brought them back to Philadelphia for his little girl to see."

Slocum nodded as he stoked the fire up.

"So I've always wanted to come up here and see the place," she concluded.

"Your father?" He stirred the small logs, and the blue flames licked upward, radiating more heat in his face.

"Dead. He died in the Civil War."

"But you kept his dream of this ranch house and land all these years?"

"Yes. I had lawyers clear the title, and I think that was what shocked Moore, how I had done all this so well."

"Tell me what your husband is like." Not looking at her, Slocum set the three-legged stand in the fire and the skillet on top of it.

"He's a kind, generous man," she said quickly.

"He's helped you pursue this dream? Financed it?" Slocum stopped his preparations and looked her in the eye.

"Of course," she said, her tone growing colder.

"Why didn't he come out here with you?"

"He . . ." She looked around to be certain they were alone. "He could never have stood the trip out here. He has had two severe heart seizures in the past year."

Slocum nodded that he had heard her. The man he disliked so much for his cowardice was disabled. So he couldn't come to help her.

"You think it is wrong I am out here alone and he's back there?" she asked.

"I told you, I don't judge what most folks do. I did about him, and I was wrong." He shook his head in deep concentration. "I just can't figure out why you want this so much."

"Slocum, I've wanted this ranch all my life."

"Yes, but there are Apaches here and there are bandits all over this territory. I can't see a woman able to hold out and ever do any good with it."

"Can I hire you to stay here?"

"No." He looked down at the dirt in front of his dusty boot toes. "One morning I'll be gone like the wild goose."

"Is there a special woman in your life? Someone that counts?"

"No, just a pocketful of jerky and canteen water. Stars for a roof and another mountain to cross." He began to place sliced bacon into the skillet, and the sizzle grew louder. The pungent aroma made his empty belly complain.

"You know I'll not be dissuaded from doing this," she said.

"Yes. That's why I came along, I guess. But I can't protect you forever."

"Then find someone who will."

"The U.S. Army isn't for hire." He shook his head in disapproval of her plans as he began to dice up potatoes. She moved closer to help him, and soon the fire's heat had warmed her.

The four of them ate breakfast and then saddled. Jones took the lead, and Slocum rode in the rear in case of trouble. The big Indian spared them little, riding up steep mountain faces and down narrow spines into a deeper canyon. Then up the broad sandy wash bottom and through the labyrinth of twisting alleyways formed by sheer high bluffs.

"Where are we at?" she asked, looking around in the saddle.

"Rancho del Norte!" Jones said as they rounded the bend and the red-tile roof of the ranch house shone in the long shafts of midday light. Slocum blinked his eyes. The hacienda still stood. One wooden gate hung in disrepair, but even the palms trees that rustled in the fresh wind stood in obedience as their owner reined in her horse and closed her eyes.

"It is still here!" she cried out aloud. Tears streamed down her cheeks as she dismounted and started running in a pigeon-toed gait toward the house.

What the hell was that crazy woman doing rushing in there? He spurred the buckskin and drew out his Winchester as he pulled alongside her. It was no time to lose caution and throw it to the wind. He had to keep her from falling into a trap.

"Let me go first," he pleaded.

"I'm certain there is nothing in there to hurt me."

"Don't be so damn certain," he said, more angry at her hardheadedness than anything else. Unable to convince her, he spurred the gelding to keep up with her.

They went through the gate and she rushed to the house. He dismounted as she swung on a porch post.

"It is here! Slocum, it is all here!"

He nodded and looked around at the rotting Red River carts, corrals in need of repair, and outbuildings ready to fall apart. But she was right. The great house looked better than he had imagined. Many windows were gone, and some ignorant souls had built a fire on the tile floor in the center of the living room, blackening the plaster ceiling between the large log rafters that spanned across it, but still . . .

There was nothing in the large kitchen but the fireplace to cook in. The iron had long ago been stripped out for arrowheads. Missing wooden furniture had no doubt served other visitors as fuel. He followed her as she rushed from room to room gushing about her ranch house. There was no sign of recent inhabitants, and they both went up the stairs to look at the second floor rooms.

"Look there." She pointed out the open double doors that

led to a balcony. "See the farmland up the canyon, and the ditches?"

He nodded and drew in a deep breath. The place had once been a palace. But the work that had to be done . . . She was hugging him and shouting, "You found my ranch!"

He never was certain, but her wet mouth was soon on his and her firm breasts drove into his chest. They sought each other until their breath was gone, and then they clung to each other as if they were drowning.

"You've got to stay and help me," she pleaded.

Her closeness was enough for anyone; her ripe body melted against him. All the unspoken promises of passion one could conjure up were there in his arms as they stood in the middle of that empty room, littered with trash and with thick dust on the once-polished tile floor.

"I'll try," he said.

"Great!" She drew his face to hers, and the generosity of her lips and hot tongue made his head swirl. Then she broke away from his mouth. "You won't regret it, Slocum. I promise you won't."

"How did it get here?" Slocum asked the Indian as they sat on the front stoop.

"In wagons they came over Iron Mountain." He tossed his head in that direction. "But the earth has broken away up there and now there is only a trail."

"Can it be made into a road?"

"Much work."

"You will have to show me that way out. Why didn't the Apaches burn this house?"

"Maybe they tried." Jones shrugged his broad shoulders. "When I was a boy, we came here and they gave us much fruit."

"What kind?"

"Peaches and dates. Grapes sometimes. The Don was a friend of the Apaches. He hired Apache women to cut hay and firewood. No one was ever mad at him. Maybe they thought he would come back if the house was still here."

"Why did he leave?"

"Americans argued with him about his . . ." Jones made a sign with his large brown hands for something he could not conjure up in words.

"His land grant?"

"Yes."

"So he left?"

Jones nodded, and then took the cigar that Slocum offered him. "This was a very special place for me to come when I was a boy."

Slocum understood the man as they smoked in silence. This had once been a very grand ranchero, and the shame was that it had ever stopped being one.

"Injuns coming!" Meyers shouted from the second-story window.

Slocum rose to his feet. He could make out their multicolored ponies and the red headbands as a half-dozen riders came off the same mountain they had. They appeared to be armed with Winchesters too. He sat down again with Jones and they both puffed on their cigars.

"What are we going to do?" Meyers screamed from upstairs.

"I guess let them have us," Slocum said, and then winked at Jones, who nodded back as they drew on their cigars.

"Aren't you afraid?" Betty shouted from the doorway. "Those Apaches are coming here."

Slocum rose and shook his head as he faced her. "Those Apaches are U.S. Army scouts. They all wear red headbands."

"Why didn't you say so?" She scowled.

"I did when you asked." He drew back as she made two fists and threatened him.

Jones had gone to greet the half-dozen riders. They dismounted and gave puzzled looks at the woman on the porch. Slocum strode over to join them.

"He says Natise left San Carlos with a band of men and women almost a week ago," Jones told him.

"He must have gone to the mountains beyond then," Slocum said.

"He is moving. He stole several horses," the scout named Rainbow said, and then made a circling with his index finger. "We have not seen any sign."

"Slocum, who is that pretty white woman?" Rainbow asked.

"Mrs. Wells from Philadelphia. She owns this place."

"What does a white woman want with such a ranch?" Rainbow then spoke the words in Apache to the others, and they shook their heads too. But obviously drawn by her beauty, they stared at her as she stood on the porch.

"Who knows about women," Jones said in Apache, and they all laughed. Their heads bobbed in agreement, but they still stole looks at her until she went inside. Meyers never ventured outside.

"We will tell Captain Lyons you have not seen them," Rainbow said, and vaulted on his horse. "We should know Slocum would be here—there was pretty woman." They laughed at his expense. "Jones, he always keeps an old fat one, so no one will steal her," Rainbow added, and they left in a cloud of dust whooping and yelling war cries.

"Ha, Rainbow doesn't know. I have new wife at McDowell." Jones wrinkled his large flat nose in defiance after them.

"A new wife?"

"Yes, she is young and pretty."

"Good, I would like to meet her some day," Slocum said as they walked back to the porch.

"No, I'll keep her at McDowell," Jones said.

15

"Where can we hire some help and get some supplies?" Betty asked Slocum. They walked the small fields that once had been irrigated by the stream of water that ran off and disappeared in the sandy bed of the canyon beyond the house.

"At Florence there are some Mexican people there who could work the land and help you clean the *casa*."

"How many will I need?" she asked.

"More than you can afford." He wanted to hold down her enthusiasm; he studied the great canyon walls above them and tried to figure out how to tell her the impossible things about this place.

"Why is that?" she asked.

"This is the heart of Apache country. There is no road in here. All the supplies must come by burro. This place is run down and—"

"How much will it cost to make a ranch out of it?"

"Several thousand dollars. If you can live that long."

"I have that much money. Then let's ask Jones; he will know about the Apaches."

"Go on, ask him." Slocum threw his hands in the air; maybe if she wouldn't listen to him she would believe the

Apache himself. Right on her heels, he trailed her to where they found Jones sitting in the shade of the white-barked sycamore.

"Mr. Jones? Can I live here and get along with the Apaches?" she asked with her hands on her hips.

"Sure," he said, and nodded his head.

"Tell her the truth!"

"She wants to be here, she can live here. How much longer are they going to run around? Even the young ones are afraid to leave the reservation." Jones bobbed his head. "Yes, the Apache days in these mountains are over."

"See there?" she said to Slocum. "Now, can you get me people and things we will need?"

"Guns?" he asked.

"Yes, guns too," she agreed.

"I'll have to have everything shipped to somewhere south, then brought in by pack train." He tried to think of the job ahead: all the things that would be required and the people necessary.

"You should go to the mine," Jones said.

"What mine?" Slocum asked.

"The one up there on Iron Mountain."

"You know about a mine?" Slocum asked her.

"No. My father was a geologist, though, and he worked for the DeVagas on their mines in Sonora. He never mentioned any mines up here, but then he might not have wanted anyone to know there was one on the property with the land grant still contested in the courts."

"That makes sense," Slocum agreed.

"I want to see the mine," she said.

"Tomorrow. We can ride there in a few hours," Jones said, and pulled his hat down for a siesta.

"Did you hear that, Mr. Meyers?" she shouted, half running over to the porch.

"No, what was it?" the man asked, coming from the house.

"There's a mine on the property."

"What kind?"

"Some kind. They dug one, it must have something valuable in it," Slocum said, seeing Jones wanted to nap. What difference did it make? They'd learn in due time what it would yield. There were a million mines in Arizona and only a few were valuable. It reminded him of Baird and their small claim which had showed some signs of gold. The one the rascal had sold out from under him while he was gone. Word was it had brought a thousand dollars. Five hundred was his share.

"Aren't you excited, Mr. Meyers?" she asked.

"Oh, yes, Mrs. Wells, I've been excited or my heart has near run away ever since we left Goldfield yesterday." He swallowed hard.

"Oh, I'm sorry."

"No." He held up his hands defensively. "I am doing things I've never done before, nor did I even dream I might do them, and I must say it is exhilarating. Thanks to both of you."

"We're riding to the mine tomorrow," Slocum said.

"Good, I've never seen a real mine." Meyers shoved his glasses back up his nose. "You must excuse me. I am going down the wash and shoot my pistol. I have been practicing sighting it. I think I'm ready to go shoot it."

"You need any help?" she asked.

"Oh, no. I shall be out of the way down there and I have found some targets to shoot at." He hoisted the tow sack in his hand.

"Sure," she said, exchanging a questioning look with Slocum.

"Good luck," Slocum said after the man.

They watched him trudge off with a sack full of clinking glass. Slocum shook his head. He had seen some peculiar things, but this was more than he could believe. The drummer was going off for pistol practice. Stranger things had happened in the world, but Slocum simply hadn't been around when they came off.

"Come, he's fine," she said, tugging on his sleeve.

"I know," Slocum said, and followed her into the house.

"I want leather-covered furniture in this room," she said, and waved her arm as if that would clean the shards of broken pottery and glass on the floor away. "Come," she said, and led him upstairs.

The stairs gritty under their soles, they reached the top floor. A cooling wind swept in the open double doors to the balcony as she ran toward them, spreading her arms wide and inhaling the freshness.

He stood a few feet behind her. The woman was intoxicated with the euphoria of finally reaching the hacienda. She turned to face him and held out her hand as if inviting him to dance. He took it and swung her around the room as if an orchestra were playing a waltz. They both must have heard the music, for she was light on her feet. He remembered growing up in Alabama—before the war. He'd danced with Kathryn like this. Fiddles now played in his head, the perfume of magnolias in the air. Why, he'd forgotten what they even smelled like until that moment. He hadn't seen a magnolia in twenty years, let alone smelled one.

They stopped dancing. Her mouth became a vessel for his. He held her so hard he feared he would break a rib, but he couldn't get enough. His hand traced over and felt her proud breasts; she sighed. There would be no stopping this time.

His hands trembled as he untied a bedroll and threw it across the floor. She kneeled beside him. Her eyes glazed over as she helped him undo the buttons on his shirt and slip it off her shoulders. He pushed away the thin straps of her chemise, and then gazed at the firm breasts capped with pink nipples.

Then he kissed them until they hardened. Finally filled with a rage to possess her, he fought his pants away.

In the smoke of their pleasure, she sprawled on the blankets and pulled him after her. Between her smooth long legs the gates of paradise opened, and he plunged into her. Breathless, they both fought for escape from the whirlpool that sucked them inward, deeper and deeper, until she cried and collapsed under him. Braced to not crush her, he felt the last throes of passion fly away. Then the wind coming in the open doorway swept across his sweaty skin and turned the droplets to icicles.

"Hold me," she cried, and closed her eyes.

He managed to get a blanket free and pulled it over their chilling nakedness to hold some heat in. Her back curled to him, he hugged her against his chest.

"Oh, Slocum. It has been years."

"Like wine worth waiting for."

"I can't recall—thank you." She reached back and patted him on the leg.

He listened. There were shots. Meyers was shooting. Not just in rapid succession, but deliberate, individual shots. Maybe he would learn after all. Slocum hugged her against him. Time to get up and start cooking supper. But who cared?

16

"What kind of a mine is it?" she asked as they dismounted and she hurried through the waist-high dried weeds toward the entrance.

"Watch for damn rattlers," Slocum scolded her. "They go inside there to be cool during the daytime."

"Are you teasing me—" She stopped and stood perfectly still. The unmistakable dry click of a nearby sidewinder froze everyone. The dry rattling grew more intense. Even Jones turned cold-stone serious, and began to search around his feet with hardly a movement of his head.

"Don't move!" Slocum shouted to her. She could be only inches from the snake. The unmistakable sound was one that he knew well enough. Somewhere close by, coiled under a bush or rock, was the creature. Slocum took careful steps in her direction with his Colt in hand. An overturned handcart lay on its side to her right. Was it under that?

"Stand perfectly still until we locate him," he warned her as he drew closer. He looked all around on the ground, any second expecting the explosion of the unseen coiled viper. "It won't strike unless you move."

"I think he's to my right," she said in a halting whisper.

"Be still," he said, unable to locate the serpent. Then the culprit moved, and he saw the pale brown form matching the desert floor as it slithered along sideways, the forked tongue testing the air as it went.

His shot threw dust and dirt over the both of them as he jumped and herded her back. She yipped, and then folded into his left arm.

"He's dead," Slocum said.

"Oh, thank God." Her face was paling under the brown tan. Her breasts rose and fell under the shirt as she gasped for air. Finally she eased herself from his hold and stood up. She bent over and used her knees for a brace as she breathed deeply.

"You all right?" he asked.

"I'll be fine in a minute or so."

"Take your time. Jones has a pine knot to use for a torch," he said as the Indian strode by and the cautious Meyers came close on his heels.

Satisfied the entrance was snake free, Jones squatted down and ignited the pitch-smelling club with a lucifer. With it blazing at last, he rose, holding it up, and looked over at them impatiently.

"I've never been in a mine before," Meyers said.

"There will be bats in here," Slocum said, bringing up the rear.

"How big?"

"Oh how big, Jones? Like eagles?"

"Some are," the Indian said, stooping to save his head from the low ceiling and holding the blazing torch up to illuminate the tunnel. Forced to bend over too, Slocum observed the tunnel wasn't built for tall men like him and Dirty Shirt.

"What kind of mine is it?" Meyers asked.

"Danged if I know," Slocum said, looking back at the bright entrance growing smaller with each step inside. Someone had timbered the sections not blasted out of whole rock, and they'd even laid a track for the dump cars. This was some mine operation, and he was impressed.

"There is the end," Jones said as the room grew large and everyone could stand up.

Slocum looked carefully at the walls. The stink of the burning pitch burned the lining of his nose as he bent down and lifted some chunks of rock. It was too dark in there to tell much. He didn't like the stale air of mines, and this one reminded him of why he didn't work in them for a living.

"Take some samples, we can have them assayed in Florence," he told them all.

"Ready?" Jones asked a few moments later, holding the light as the rest straightened with rocks in their hands.

"I'm anxious to see these in the light," she said, hurrying to keep up with Slocum as they walked back toward the entrance.

"You know much about rocks?" Slocum asked.

"A little."

"That's all I know, but whatever they got out of here was valuable enough for them to invest all the time and resources they spent on it. Jones, did you ever hear what they mined?"

"Maybe gold."

"Is what I'm carrying gold?" Meyers asked.

"Could be a pure chunk, but more than likely it has some flake gold in it and needs to be crushed and separated," Slocum assured the man.

At last, grateful to be outdoors again, Slocum examined the rocks in his hand. They looked shiny enough to be worth something.

"What do you think?" he asked her.

"Might be some silver in them." She shrugged, and then Meyers turned one of his samples around letting the sunlight glint on the wire gold. Fine yellow spiderwebs ran through the one side of the rock. They all began nodding their heads at the discovery.

"It's gold, all right. You may be very rich," Slocum said to her.

"Good, then I can hire who I want."

Meyers pushed his glasses up his nose and shook his head. "My, my, this is interesting. My first trip into a mine and I come out with gold."

"You recall me asking why a banker wanted your deed? I think I can answer that now," Slocum said to her. As far as he was concerned, that was the answer, and she wouldn't have to look any further unless there was another mine on the place.

"But how would he know there was gold up here?" she asked.

"I'd say he took samples from the mine."

"Isn't that trespassing?"

"It is called high-grading, I think, but yes, it is trespassing."

"What can she do about it?" Meyers asked.

"Post guards around the clock is all I know."

"I'd rather not do that job," the shorter man said, walking gingerly through the dried weed patch toward their horses.

"Did I hear you shooting?" Jones asked with a grin. "You don't want to sit up here and run off high-graders?"

"No! I couldn't hit a circus elephant with this gun." Meyers shook his head and then mounted his small horse. "You better find a better gunman than me to guard this mine."

"Did you point and shoot it?" Slocum asked as he helped Betty to mount up.

"I haven't got the hang of it yet, but I'm buying more shells when I get to Florence," he said, and booted his horse toward the west and the trail they'd come up on.

"I wonder if there is very much gold," she said, looking intently at the entrance.

"Hard to say," he told her, looking across the desert floor that lay to the south from their lofty perch on the side of Iron Mountain. Thirty or so miles south, the Gila River snaked through the arid land on its westward course to the Colorado. Florence lay beyond the Gila. Jones took the lead, and Slocum captured the packhorse rope to take him in tow. If her mine was rich, he could understand the banker hoping to buy it cheap from someone ignorant of its existence.

"What are you thinking?" she asked, reining up her horse to wait for him.

"I think I need to pay this banker Moore a visit in Picket Post. I have some questions to ask him."

"What good will it do?"

"I'm not sure, but there needs to be some answers."

"You know about a banker in Picket Post named Moore?" he asked Jones aloud as they started down the steep trail off the face of the mountain.

"He pays some men to ride for him."

"Who?"

"One is a Ute called Two Feathers who says he is an Apache. Two breeds and a lazy Mexican from Tubac called Carlos Jiminez. The boss is a short guy called Gates."

"What do they do for him?"

"I think they scare people who owe the bank money."

"Nice-sounding folks." Slocum shook his head; he could dislike the man even before their first meeting.

"I never met them," she said with a visible shudder of her shoulders.

"How do you know all this?" Slocum asked loud enough that Jones could hear above the protest of saddle leather and their horses scrambling on the rocks for their footing.

"I caught some bronco Apaches near their place. One of the captives knew this Two Feathers, and said if I wouldn't kill him he would show me where I could get three more to turn in." Jones paused and sharply reined his horse to stop him from going too fast downhill.

"They won't pay for Utes at Ft McDowell, and those breeds never were on the reservation. But me and that boy squatted down and I watched them for a day, and then this Moore came and gave them their money. He tells that man who leads them, Gates, what to do."

"What is Gates like?"

"I call him a rooster. A little man who rides a big black stud and has a big sombrero from Chihuahua."

Betty shook her head; obviously she had not seen Moore's army. Slocum reined up his horse to give her a chance to stop a moment on the switchback and get her bearings. The way downhill was steep as a cow's face, and he understood her apprehension, but their horses were surefooted and shod.

"Is there a better way in and out of here?" she asked.

"The road to the mine and on to the ranch broke off in an earthquake."

"Which way was it?"

"I think east of here," he said to her.

"Can it be rebuilt?"

"I hope so," he said with a smile for her as she booted her horse to half-slide a few feet and then pick his way down the sheer trail.

Later, on the bottom of the mountain, Slocum wiped his gritty forehead on his sleeve and sat the buckskin, satisfied the worst was over. She gave him the reins to her mount, and headed on foot around the corner in the dry wash. Lickety-split, Meyers took off the other way.

"So you didn't get any bounty out of them?" he asked Jones, pounding his saddlehorn with his palm.

"No. I saw that Carlos Jiminez there. You remember him? Packed for the Army one time. He was always sleeping or getting someone else to load his mules. Then he got an Apache wife and he made her do all his work. She finally ran away.''

"I think I recall him. Them breeds dangerous?"

"No, they're dumb boys, but Two Feathers and Gates could be.''

"I'll watch out for them."

"We could scare them away," Jones said with a sly grin in the corner of his brown lips.

"How is that?" He frowned at the man.

"Dress up in sheets and really scare the hell out of them."

"We might get shot too." He wasn't going to take a chance; they might not be that ghost-shy.

"We only have to empty their guns." Jones shared a wink with him. "Be plenty big time."

"We'll see about it," he said, wondering how scared you could make riffraff like that. It might be worth a try. Betty returned and mounted up; soon Meyers joined them, and they rode south for Florence.

Ralph paused and then drew back inside the haberdashery. That was the Wells woman riding with four—no, with three men right up Main Street. What was she doing in Florence anyway? Obviously his boys had not found them in the mountains. Who was the Indian riding with them? Moore had seen the big man someplace before, maybe in Picket Post or Goldfield. An Indian that size was unusual. The drummer was the man wearing the derby, and the big Stetson was on the wanted man—Slocum. They all were in Florence for some reason.

"Something wrong, Mr. Moore?" the merchant asked, sounding concerned.

"No, Mr. Caruthers. I was simply checking my wallet to be certain I had not forgotten anything." To make his point he drew it out and flipped through the leather binder, then replaced it in his inside coat pocket with a nod. "Everything

is fine. Have a good day.'' He tipped his hand to his derby
and went out again.

They were a half block away when he started up the boardwalk after them. He intended to follow them and see what
they were up to. Then he stopped, his heart beating in his
throat—they were reining before Blanton and McCraory's assay office. Why there? Damn them, someone had told that
bitch about the mine. He clenched his fist so hard at his side
that he shuddered under his coat. To be less conspicuous, he
stepped back into the shadows of the porch at the Shamrock
Saloon. The stale smell of cigar smoke and raw liquor drifted
out through the swinging doors. The odor made his stomach
roil as he decided what to do next. Change the samples? He
might be able to do that.

Where was Gates? Obviously he had not taken up their
tracks and had instead gone back to the ranch, or maybe they'd
left before Gates and the men got there. Damn, what a mess.
If word got out about that mine's value, he would never be
able to get rid of her and have the phony DeVaga sign it over.
Things had gone too far already. Somehow he had to get the
woman to sign it over to him herself. The deed didn't even
bear her husband's name.

Coughing as he jammed his shoulder to the door facing and
considering his expanding problems, he felt close to puking.
He had never mentioned the mine to her. She had not asked
about it, nor had she ever spoken of it, though he'd listened
closely to her words. No, she'd been ignorant of the mine's
existence when she arrived in Arizona.

Good mines were not easy to come by. But he owned others, like the Lady Luck. The DeVaga ore he'd had assayed in
Florence could have come from his Lady Luck mine as far as
anyone knew in the office. They'd thought he'd had it assayed
for the purpose of making a loan.

A cold chill ran up the backs of his arms as he recalled

strangling that gambler Baird who'd sold him the Lady Luck. That lying no-account tinhorn had showed him an assay report from some Tombstone mine ore, not samples from the Lady Luck. They had been rich as hell in silver. Why, he'd paid the liar fifteen hundred dollars for the mine and the thing was worthless. When he'd learned the depths of the man's deception, he'd ridden a horse into the ground to catch the gambler sleeping in a bedroll between Phoenix and Wickenburg on the Hassayampa River.

If he hadn't happened to see Baird's fancy horse picketed near the river, he'd never've stopped in the predawn light. The gambler was sleeping like a baby when Moore got his hands on his throat; both his thumbs shoving into that no good cheat's Adam's apple. Baird soon stopped gurgling. That taught him a lesson he'd never forget—no one messes with Ralph Moore.

Then he robbed him, and dumped him face down in the shallow river as if he had drowned in six inches of water. He cut his horse loose, a bald-face horse with a watch eye. It was a good high-priced son of a gun, but too easy to trace. He recovered almost twelve hundred dollars from Baird's pockets. The rest he had no doubt lost gambling.

Where were Wells and her gang going next? He saw Slocum and her come out of the assay office and then ride on. He needed to know a lot more about their business. That mine would solve all the problems of shortages in his bank. He had a complicated system of phony bank notes supporting his business. But if a new examiner come in and found them, it could crumble his empire. He drew his sharp upper teeth across his lower lip. They had to be stopped at any cost.

17

"Jones, go see if you can find any of the ex-scouts we used to ride with," Slocum said. "We can use a couple of them. Tell them it pays fifty bucks and grub." He looked toward Betty for confirmation.

Her head bobbed in affirmation as she sat on her horse. He drew in a deep breath, still not convinced that she was doing the right thing by spending all this money on men and equipment. But it was her money. So what the hell should he worry about. But he did all the same.

"Tell them they may have to sleep with a rifle," he added.

Jones agreed in silence, and then reined his horse into the traffic to leave. He would find some good men if they were around. The chances were good some were still around the area, since the Army had laid off several. Slocum turned back to her.

"What are your plans?" he asked.

"I'm going over to that bank over there and hope there isn't another Moore in it," she said.

Across the street from them, the First National Bank looked official enough, with gold letters on the window. Though he had never parted its doors, it looked stable enough for her to do business in. The chances of her meeting another greedy banker like Moore were slight in his judgment.

"What good will that do?" he asked.

"I have a bank draft in this valise that we didn't let float away. And I will also have my banker transfer more money here to cover the expenses we incur."

"It is going to cost big bucks to do all this," he said privately to her, standing on the ground beside her leg. She needed the option to back out. He was not convinced the idea of a woman running an empire was at all logical—at least in the Superstitions.

"I want to do this. I am no child, Slocum."

"Yes, ma'am."

Scowling at his reply, she booted him in the chest with her toe and stirrup. "That formality isn't necessary. Where are you going next?"

"I'm going to hire some mule teams and wagons. See about some cattle for your ranch. I'm also looking for a man who might work that mine for you."

"Good." She motioned with a head toss. "Meet us at the hotel. I'll get you a room. We'll go to supper at six p.m."

"Meyers," he said, after acknowledging he'd heard her plans. "Don't you let her out of your sight."

"I won't." The man sat up straight in the saddle.

"Thanks," she said softly, and shared a private look with Slocum.

He mounted the buckskin in a bound and set him into a trot. Standing in the stirrups, he reined the gelding around the vehicles that crowded the street. Teams of wagons with oxen and mules were hitched along with freighters waiting to unload or move on.

He reached the cantina in the *barrio* district, and hitched his horse at the empty rack. It was siesta time; he'd be lucky to find his man. If he hadn't gone home to Chihuahua, he should be ready to do some ore hauling. Besides, he would know of possible people around there to work the ranch for her.

"Villa here?" he asked the bartender polishing glassware behind the bar.

"He's upstairs."

"Go tell him that . . ."

A small man with a chest like a banty rooster came down the stairs. His shirt was so white and starched, it hurt Slocum's eyes in the dark saloon interior.

'What kind of a gringo rides up and disturbs my siesta?''

"Pancho!" Slocum shouted as the man shook his head in dismay at the discovery, and then smiled as they rushed to hug each other.

"You mean a jealous husband has not killed you?" Villa asked, looking him over from head to toe.

"Not yet, and even you are alive."

"I am a very careful man. What brings you back here?"

"I have a mine that needs to be worked. Ore that needs to be hauled. You are the man I could think of to do that."

"Which mine?" Villa asked as he waved the bartender over with a bottle and glasses.

"The DeVaga Mine."

"How much money is there in it for me?"

"Ten percent of the gold to run the mine, and ten dollars a ton to haul the ore to Globe in your wagons."

"That is a long haul." He shook his head as if disappointed about the distance.

"Those wagons will rot down sitting out there," Slocum said. "I have seen no one rush in here and make you such a generous offer."

"True, but this mine is in Apache territory." Villa put his hand on Slocum's shoulder and gave him a serious look.

"The Army has them all on the San Carlos or McDowell reservations."

"Sit, my friend, and we will discuss this matter further." He motioned to a chair and set the bottle from the barkeep on the table.

"Your chance to make some good money." Slocum pushed his hat up with his thumb and eased back in the chair.

"Who owns this mine?" Villa poured them drinks in the glasses.

"A Mrs. Wells." He took the drink from him.

"You work for her?" Villa made a face as if he was impressed.

"Yes. She is around thirty, attractive, and very cold."

"Ha! You have been in her bed, no?" He raised the glass in a salute to Slocum. A sly knowing grin spread over his handsome face as he waited for the response.

"No."

"Damn, you don't even lie good anymore." Villa shook his head in vehement disbelief.

"The mine offer?"

"What can I do but accept it?" He shrugged his shoulders in defeat.

"Good. No high-graders," Slocum said, pressing his point. Ore haulers sometimes pulled over en route to the smelter, and took the richer ore and ditched it beside the road for their later use. He wanted no part of such thievery.

"No high-graders," Villa agreed.

"We need to send some men with teams, slips, and dynamite to reopen the road to the mine first."

"In the morning. Who pays?"

"She will. I'll have some riflemen go along and be sure they aren't surprised." He tried another sip of the cactus juice. It was still too fiery for his taste.

"How bad is the road?" Villa leaned on the table with his elbows, his dark eyes like chunks of coal.

"It probably will take a week's work to get it passable."

"Good, I can grease and work over my other wagons in the meanwhile," Villa said. "I will also send to Sonora for some miners."

"I also need a couple tough vaqueros who want to work."

"When do you need them?"

"When the cattle arrive."

"When is that?"

"Perhaps in a week. I have to buy them first."

Slocum rose to his feet, ignoring the man's doubtful look. "I'll know more about that later. Keep your mustache waxed, Villa."

The man used the web of his hand to smooth the jet-black growth. He smiled at Slocum and then settled down. He raised the glass and toasted him.

"Gracias, amigo," Villa said. "To a very rich mine, no?"

"I know you'll get the gold out for her."

"No problem. She can make the payroll and expenses?"

"Oh, yes. I need to go line up the supplies. I'll also need two families to work the farmland."

"I can supply them." Villa puffed out his chest and sat up straight, taking in more of the cactus extract.

"I'll need some of their women to work at the house." He set his own glass down. Good whiskey was hard to beat; he would appreciate the next drink more after this stuff.

"An ideal job for some people I know," Villa said. "The Carteras family will be ready when you want them to leave."

"Get a string of burros for me too. We need to pack in to the main ranch with them until that road can be rebuilt on the far side."

"This Wells woman, she is here?" Villa's dark eyes gleamed. He looked like he had hatched a new plan.

"She's at the Grand Hotel. You can meet her in the morning for breakfast at eight a.m."

"Done, amigo. I will be there. Where do you want the burros?"

"Green's Mercantile at daylight with some packers."

"You are certainly spending much money."

"That's what the lady wants," he said, and shook the man's hand. Villa was a real businessman; if the mine could produce enough ore, she could ranch with the proceeds until the angels came to call. Pancho also knew the right men to pick for miners and teamsters. The mine's operation would be taken care of.

Slocum rode the horse back and placed him in the livery. Then he crossed the street to the empty holding pens, the yellow tan dirt swept clean by the winds. The Paterson Commission Company's sign swung back and forth in the afternoon gale. He stepped through the doorway, and two handmade boots shifted from the desk top to the floor.

Slocum's and Todd Paterson's introductions were short. They shook hands, and the cow buyer indicated a chair for Slocum to take.

"What's your business in Florence, Slocum?"

"I need two-fifty solid mouth cows with calves at side."

"Big order," Todd said, twisting the end of his gray mustache in deep thought.

"Too big an order for you, I'll ride to Tucson."

"No need in that. I've got a good set coming out of Texas."

"How much?"

"Fifteen."

"Twelve dollars and no broken mouths. Must have calves trailing them." Paterson had a piece of red cedar between his knees and a jackknife to whittle with as they talked. He occasionally punctuated his speech with a spit in the spittoon beside his barrel-back chair.

"Whew, you could hurt a man. It is damn hard to get cattle up here that cheap."

"That's what I'm ordering," Slocum said, and reset the hat on his head to rise. "That's what I'll pay."

"Hold up a minute. There's lots of money involved in a deal like this."

"Mrs. Wells can handle it. Check with the First National Bank, she has an account with them. You get the right cattle—"

"Who is she?" Paterson frowned.

"Mrs. Betty Wells."

"You her foreman?" He spat in the can.

"Yes. When will my cattle be here?" He was ready to leave. The long shadows of sundown from the open doorway were crossing the gritty wood floor. It would be six o'clock soon and he hated to keep a lady waiting.

"Two weeks, but—"

"Solid mouths."

"I heard you."

He crossed the street and noticed a man make a funny face at him in the distance, then duck into a store. Where had he seen that person before? Was it a coincidence or had the man intended to avoid him? Slocum wondered about the incident as he hurried to the hotel two blocks away with ten million things to tell Betty. He looked over his shoulder. No one followed him. He still felt in his gut that it was all wrong to spend this money on such a wild venture—especially for a woman. And someone was spying on him. But who?

He crossed the lobby and noticed her coming down the stairs. She wore a new blue dress that molded her willowy figure and made his guts roil, as he recalled the package under it. On her heels came Meyers with his coat open and his gun exposed. The man obviously was taking the guard business seriously. Good. Slocum could hardly tell what to expect. Somehow he felt that all this business wouldn't get by Moore, not if he realized he was missing a real opportunity.

"Good evening," she said with a smile, and took his arm. "Your mine manager will meet you for breakfast here at eight."

"What's his name?"

"Villa, his friends call him Pancho. He is a little bandy Mexican, but he can get lots done. I hired him to manage it for you for ten percent of the mine's gold and ten dollars a ton to haul the ore to Globe."

"Is that a fair price?"

"No, but it is a good enough deal you shouldn't get robbed or cheated. Besides, I trust Pancho," he said in a half whisper as the waiter showed them to their seats.

"Good enough for me," she said as he seated her.

"We'll send the road builders out with guards tomorrow."

"My head's spinning," she said, putting the linen napkin in her lap. "Ernest, I guess we better order some food."

"Yes, ma'am," Meyers said, and ducked behind the menu.

Slocum ordered the steak, beans, and potatoes. Meyers followed suit, and she selected ham. He frowned at her selection, but it was her stomach.

"Not a good thing to order?" she asked when the waiter left.

"I have no idea." He leaned closer to her. "I have a family to work the ranch, two vaqueros coming, and two hundred and fifty cows and calves."

She blinked her eyes and frowned. "All this afternoon?"

"Your empire is coming."

"Ernest, did you hear all this?"

"Yes, I did."

"Soon we will have a ranch and a working mine. Isn't it grand?"

"Yes, sure. I guess you won't need me with all that help," the man said.

"Why, Ernest, you and Slocum have saved my life. There will be a job for you two at my ranch for your lifetime."

"Yes, ma'am."

The food came and their conversation stopped. Slocum had a million questions to ask her, but they would wait. He glanced around the room. No one acted as if they were intent on him—good, he was mighty visible doing all this. Perhaps he should ride up to Goldfield and see if Milly knew anything else about Moore and his bunch.

"Mr. Slocum," the waiter said, interrupting his thoughts between bites.

"Yes?"

"A Mr. Jones on the porch outside sent word that he needs to speak to you, sir."

"Thank you. Excuse me," he said, rising, realizing Jones would never come inside hotel's table-clothed restaurant. He hurried outside, and found the Indian leaning against the wall in the growing darkness.

"I hired Joe Clayton and Walt Shuffer."

"Good men. They leave at daybreak with the road crew. Have them meet me at Green's store and I'll get them grub and ammunition."

"What else?" Jones asked.

"We'll need twenty good saddle horses for this ranch."

"I can buy them cheap from the reservation Apaches."

"Cow ponies, not wind-broke nags," Slocum cautioned him, making certain Jones had no intention of buying some broken-down bangtails.

"Plenty good horses. Cost about ten dollars in silver apiece."

Slocum checked his pockets. He had less than forty on him.

"Stay here. I'll go get the money."

He hurried back and slipped into his seat. "I need two hundred dollars for saddle horses. Jones is going tonight for them."

"Here," she said, digging in her purse. She handed him the currency.

The folded paper money was not the answer. No Apache would ever take the like for his good horses. He thanked her, pocketed the bills, and hurried outside.

"What's the matter?" Jones asked as he joined him in a fast pace to cross the street to the mercantile.

"All she has are bills. We can change them over at Green's."

Soon, the silver money in a sack, Jones mounted up after promising to go by and tell the two ex-scouts to show up at dawn. Before he let him go, Slocum reminded him again to buy sound horses. Then Jones rode off down the shadowy street. Slocum watched for a moment from the porch. No sign of anything. He went back and finished his meal.

Mrs. Wells paid for their meals and the three of them adjourned to her room. Slocum stood by the window and studied the areas lit by businesses, spreading yellow lights into the street. She and Meyers discussed the meal and the very dry ham she had ordered.

There was that same man again crossing over from Green's. It was him, all right. He recognized the hat even. The one who'd had the funny look on his face. Slocum was ready to ask her to try to identify him, but he was quickly gone again into the shadows on the porches.

18

"He's buying what?" Ralph asked the cattle dealer. He couldn't believe the man's words—buying cattle for what purpose? Where was this gambler getting his money? That woman's pockets? No doubt she was backing him—but a live-stock operation would be impossible up there with the Indians and all that.

"He told me he wanted two hundred and fifty head of cows and calves. No short mouths and all sound," Todd Paterson said. "And we're to make the deal in two weeks."

"What in hell's name is he going to do with them?"

"Mr. Moore, at twelve dollars a head, he can milk them, separate the cream, and sell butter for all I care."

"He say how he would get the money to pay you?" Ralph turned his ear to carefully hear the man's response. He watched an attractive woman pass before the commission house door, and appraised her figure.

"He said a Mrs. Wells had the money at the First National Bank."

"Did you talk to her?"

"You saying this deal is sour?" Paterson arched his thin eyebrows.

Moore shrugged. What in hell's name would they do with that many cows? Drive them into the Superstitions? They were crazy. The Apaches would have a barbecue every night. Besides, with cattle prices the way they were . . . Wait. Those reservations full of Indians would be buying beef for a long time to come. Was that their plan? Stock the ranges and sell to the agency?

He wished an answer to his telegram had come back. The one he'd sent off to Kansas earlier in the day. If there was a good enough reward on Slocum he might even jump him himself. He needed to get her out of town and then dispose of her body after she signed the deed over to him. He figured the only way he could take the ranch was to force her to sell it to him.

"Dammit, Moore, where you rushing off to?" Paterson swore after him. "You saying the cow deal is no good?"

"You better check on her credit!" Ralph said over his shoulder. She must have all the money in the world, buying that many cattle and hiring men like Slocum. He certainly wouldn't work as cheap as Gates. Keeping an eye out for any of the four of them, he hurried down the boardwalk for the telegraph office. There had to be an answer to all this, and he was the only one smart enough to figure it all out.

It would help if Gates was there to snoop around and learn what else Slocum was up to. Luckily he'd watched the man come out of Paterson's office. There had to be some sense to buying all this cattle. If he hadn't observed Slocum leaving Paterson's and gone to ask the trader, he wouldn't know a thing. Still, the dead whore Milly had said he was wanted in Kansas. That had to be an ace in the hole.

What else had Slocum done in town? His spy in Green's, the Fulpher boy, Luke, hadn't seen a thing of him or her in the store. They would need to buy their supplies there. Maybe he could find out something about his wire. He stepped inside the telegraph office, and to his disgust saw an oaf was ahead of him.

"Ten cents a word," the clerk under the celluloid cap said to the simpleton standing before the counter.

"I want her to know that I love her and want her to come out here and marry me," the towheaded youth in overalls said.

"Be right with you, Mr. Moore," the clerk said. He turned back to the youth. "I love you is thirty cents."

"Oh, I've got that much money. The part about would you come out here and marry me is next."

"Would you come out here and marry me is next." The clerk counted off on his fingers. "That's a dollar."

"I don't really need 'is next,' just Sam Sloan is good enough. That'll be how much?"

"A dollar-thirty."

"Will she get it soon?" The youth was counting his pennies and the small change from his pocket. The process proved painfully slow, for he lost count twice and was forced to start over.

"Soon as I can send it to her," the clerk said.

Finally, in despair, the youth looked up and shook his head. "What can we leave out? I ain't got that much money."

"How much do you have?" Moore asked, standing on one foot, then the other.

"One dollar and fifteen cents is all, sir." A blank look of disappointment flushed the youth's face as he stood holding out the money in his palm.

"Here, send it and get going." Moore handed the clerk a quarter.

"That's right nice of you, sir. I sure appreciate it and I'm sure my darling Sara will too. My name's Sam Sloan."

"Ralph Moore. Did I get a message back?" he asked the clerk, anxious to be free of the farm boy.

"You certainly did."

Ralph took the envelope, removed the yellow sheet, and carefully read the glued letters on the page.

TO: R. MOORE
FLORENCE AT
JOHN SLOCUM SOUGHT ON MURDER WARRANT
STOP ARMED AND DANGEROUS STOP FIVE HUN-
DRED DOLLARS REWARD STOP MY DEPUTY
TAKING THE TRAIN TODAY YOUR CITY STOP
LEARN DIRECTION HE GOES STOP SHERIFF MAR-
VIN COILS FT SCOTT KANSAS

Five hundred dollars. Good, he could use that. Where had Slocum gone? He was right there in Florence. This would be like taking candy from a baby. Without him around, the woman wouldn't have such a strong will and would sign over the deed. That Indian and the drummer could have their throats cut and be tossed in the Gila River outside of town.

"Anything else, Mr. Moore?"

"Yes, I need to send a wire to a man in Goldfield."

"I can do that. That was sure nice of you to pay for that young man's proposal."

"Oh, yes," he said, addressing the wire to Bobbie Gates in Goldfield.

Come to Paterson's yards in Florence at once. R. M.

"That all, sir?" the agent asked.

"Yes, I need him to come pick up some cattle from Paterson," he said to disguise his purpose, and then he paid the clerk.

Darkness had taken the street when he went outside. Where was Slocum staying? He needed to put a bullet in the man and collect the reward. If he couldn't, the Kansas deputy would. No, he wanted the five-hundred-dollar reward for himself.

•   •   •

Dawn came like a slow blanket across the land. A cool north wind stirred the loose dirt in the street and sent it circling south and drifting in little waves where the boardwalk ended at the alleyway between Green's and Merdigan's Harness and Saddle Shop.

A man called Raol was the pack train driver Villa sent. He and three boys in their teens swarmed around the burros and filled packs with the items from the store.

Then, squatted on his boot heels, Raol smoked the small butt of a roll-your-own pinched between his fingers, and nodded as Slocum carefully explained the plans in Spanish.

"Don't cross the mountain until I get there. Then we can go to the ranch. Stay close by the wagons and the men on the road crew. I should be up there in a day and take you to the ranch. You will have guards, but stay close to them."

Raol nodded, and then took the small stub from his mouth. The wind tore it from his fingers and the brown paper came apart, sending a few quick sparks. Both men rose and shook hands. The packer shifted the heavy-knit serape on his shoulders and then went to check on his boys. His *chihuahua* sombrero threatened by the wind, he tightened the strap under his chin and then began giving orders to better distribute the load on some of the burros.

Slocum was satisfied the pack train was in hand, and stepped to the corral to speak to the two former scouts. They stood with their backs to the cold wind using their saddle horses as a blocker.

"Joe," he said in greeting, and shook hands with him and the thicker-built Walt. "Good to see you two."

They made small talk about the job ahead and old times. The two men also shot glances at the store and asked about the woman. Slocum explained it was her operation. They nodded in agreement.

"I hope it is uneventful, but keep your eyes peeled for trou-

ble. There can still be a renegade or two up there that Jones
missed.''

"We'll watch over them," Walt said.

"That's why I sent for you two. We need the road to the
mine rebuilt as quick as possible so we can get supplies in
and ore wagons out as well.''

"No problem. Where did Jones go in such a hurry?''

"Up to San Carlos to buy some saddle horses," Slocum
said.

The men nodded, and after a few words of friendly conversation, Slocum left them for the store. The wagons were
being loaded with beans, rice, sugar, flour, and meal. Also iron
strap, horseshoes, nails, and coal for a blacksmith. The second
wagon carried caps, dynamite, fuses, star drills, hammers,
picks and shovels, and enough canvas to make a tent for the
men and a cook. Pots, pans, and the rest of the accessories for
two camps completed the load.

Samuel Green and his clerks were busy listing things that
Slocum had picked out for the men to take out. Meyers and
Betty stood back looking over the operation.

"Have I spent all your money?" Slocum stopped and
looked at her.

"We need these things?''

"Yes." Then he compressed his lips. The mine better work
or the lady would be in the poorhouse. Slocum went over and
directed Raol to start his burros for the mountains. Then he
went down the list that Meyers had checked off and he nodded
his approval to the wagon men.

Villa's men made certain their loads were secure, and then
waved to him they were ready to leave. Juan, who headed the
teamsters, spoke to the ex-scouts, and soon they were all moving out. Joe and Walt rode off at the rear as Slocum stood on
the porch wondering what he had forgotten to send along with
them. Sand stinging his face, he watched them head northward

for the ferry across the Gila River. He waited until they were out of sight in the dust storm. Satisfied, he turned and started inside the mercantile.

The glass crashed from the impact of a bullet striking. He dove for his life. Mrs. Wells's screams shattered the morning as he rolled up in a ball, then like a cat sprang to his feet behind the counter. With no shooter in sight, he tried to decide where the bullet came from. Gun drawn, he rushed to the front door with a shout for her to get back. A vision of her ashen face was all he saw as he tried to locate the shooter.

"I can't see him," Meyers said from the edge of the doorway opposite him. His Colt was in hand, and for a long moment Slocum had to control a grin. The man was ready for trouble.

"He was near the livery. Probably gone by now," Slocum said.

"What do you want to do?" Meyers asked, still carefully searching the street and beyond for a shooter.

"I'm going to run for the livery. I'll stop at that wagon."

"I'll cover you."

"Good." With that Slocum raced in a crooked path for the farm wagon, finding cover without drawing any fire, and then made an all-clear sign for Meyers's sake. He could not see anything out of place as he studied the dark buildings that were still out of the sun's reach.

"Who wants you dead?" Meyers asked, breathing hard as he joined him at the rear wheel.

"Too many folks, but none I know here."

"You weren't kidding about me guarding her, were you?"

"No, I was serious." Where had the shooter gone? No telling. By this time he had slipped off into the darkness. Slocum needed to find the shell if the shooter had ejected it; the report had sounded like a rifle.

"You think she's safe with me?" Meyers asked.

"She may be more your responsibility from here on."

"Why?" he asked, carefully rolling the cylinder of his gun around so the hammer fell on the empty cylinder.

"If someone is after me personally, I don't need her hurt."

"Who shot at you?" Betty demanded, joining them.

"A hungry hunter," he said, holstering his own Colt.

"Don't be silly," she said, looking around with distaste. "Can we leave here?"

"Not yet. Take her to the hotel," he said to Meyers. "I'll be along."

"Where are you going?" she demanded.

"Go on. Meyers can take care of things." With that said, and not wanting to argue with her, he set out in a run for the side of the barn.

The gusty wind had saved him. Either in the form of grit in the shooter's eyes or something else. It was too easy a shot to miss him at that distance. The cold blast struck his face and threatened his hat. He hugged his canvas duster around him. Where had the backshooter gone?

19

No cartridge in sight. Though Slocum searched carefully where he felt the gunman had been standing, he had no success. Appraising the situation, Slocum stood beside the stables looking back at the store across the street. Green and a young clerk were nailing boards over the windowless door. He felt convinced the shooter had been at this exact spot.

"You hear the shot?" he asked the stable hand inside the office. Grateful to be out of the cold, he held his hands out to the small sheet-iron stove. The radiant heat began to warm his face and seek the front of his cord pants.

"Rolled me out of bed," the sleepy-eyed youth said between sips of coffee from a stained mug he cradled in his hands.

"Didn't see anything?"

"No. It was still dark in here and I wasn't anxious to run out and get my head shot off."

"I don't blame you. Did you hear where the shot came from?"

"I was sound asleep, but it was close by." The youth shook his head as if he had considered it.

"Any toughs ride in here lately?"

121

"Not none that look like a backshooter. Aw, there's lot's of folks come through here all the time, but I ain't seen no hardcases in a while."

"Thanks," Slocum said, and left the office to face the north wind.

Villa would be meeting with Mrs. Wells soon. Slocum had better go and be there for that meeting. He looked up and down the near-empty street. A man with a badge crossed from Green's store, looking like he wanted something.

"Hold up!" the man shouted, the sound nearly lost in the sharp wind.

The lawman asked who Slocum was and what he knew about the shot, which wasn't much. He frowned a lot at having to be up at this early hour, and allowed how he didn't like guns going off in his jurisdiction. Slocum agreed with the man, explained what had happened, then hurried on to the hotel.

Ralph stood in the kitchen and listened to the sharp whistle at the corners of the adobe house. His 38-40 Winchester leaned against the wall. The steaming coffee misted his stuffy nose. Overnight he had taken a cold, and now his eyes were watering excessively. He'd probably caught it from that damn Theresa. The blasted wind and his watery eyes had made him miss the damn gambler. He knew the man had dived back inside on his own power—not from the force of the heavy lead bullet. Luckily, Moore had managed to slip away quickly enough so that no one had seen him.

He blew his nose into a handkerchief, wiped his nostrils, and then folded the handkerchief back and inserted it into his hind pocket. His men should get the telegram and be at Paterson's by sundown, if they made it back to Goldfield from the mountains. They might have gone back to his ranch, not finding the woman and the others in the Superstitions. In that case he would have to ride over there and get them.

"Ah, my baby is up," Theresa said, and rushed across the floor to hug him.

He allowed her to press her voluptuous body to his. She wore only a thin nightdress, and the curves of her mature body molded around him. Her small hands rubbed his chest, and then she pursed her pouty lips for a kiss. One thing about Theresa, she was no stupid woman who had to be forced into sex and reminded of her duties to him. He grinned to himself—she wanted it. Her mouth tasted like stale honey when he kissed her—but still the sweetness was there.

"Do you have to leave?" she purred as her hand explored the front of his pants.

"Not soon."

"Good, put the coffee down. The house is too cold and my sheets are still warm. Why didn't you wake me when you woke up? I would have cared for you then." She led him to the bed.

A good alibi—she didn't know he had been up. No one knew about his missed aim: a five-hundred-dollar shot. The Fulpher boy had told him they were packing to leave and had a large order. Two large ore wagons full and a pack train of burros—enough to stock a city. Or worse, feed and equip a large number of miners.

Theresa had already undone his pants and unbuttoned his underwear and slipped it from his shoulders. The cooler air of the dark bedroom washed over his bare skin. A foxy smile was on her face as her hot hand cradled his scrotum; he drew in his breath, raising to his toes. He tore his underwear off inside out, and they leaped onto the feather bed.

In a flash, he was between her parted legs and pumping home his throbbing manhood. His intent was to drive her head through the limed oak headboard of the great bed. The billowy feather mattress beneath them rolled like a tempest-tossed sea; her hands raced over his bare skin.

Her cries of pleasure sounded like a gull he recalled from the Gulf. With her lips parted and the even white teeth exposed, she pleaded with him aloud for more and more. And he gave it to her. Until she fainted away and then came back mumbling for even more. Blind with his intent, he swirled in a world of cloud-like pleasure until, out of breath, he paused, withdrew from her, and then rolled her over on her stomach.

"Yes!" she cried as she rose on her knees under him, exposing her derriere for his purposes. With her guidance, he drove the nail home. Ropes under them protested and he clutched her long breasts and relentlessly piled again and again into her. Then they finally both fell into a spent heap on a sheet soaked with their fluids and slept.

Slocum found his bunch in the restaurant. Villa, with his raven black hair plastered flat and shiny in the light, was his usual pompous self as he waved his hands like the leader of a band to explain things to Betty. Slocum took a seat and drew a nod from everyone as the man continued his story.

"I met this man Slocum," he said, acknowledging him, "in Chihuahua years ago. We are like brothers, no?"

Slocum agreed with a nod. The man was not going to tell Betty about the Martinez sisters—he knew that.

"Bandits were stealing the ore I was being paid to haul. I was a very small businessman then and only had two wagons. So I hired this gringo to help me stop the banditos. Ah, Señora Wells, in a week those bandits were sleeping with lambs in heaven, no? And my business was saved."

She nodded, and then carefully went back to picking at her food.

"How many years ago was that?" Villa asked, turning to face Slocum.

Slocum shook his head. "We've known each other for many years."

"There was a time in Mexico we stole back the teams that rustlers took."

"I am certain that Mrs. Wells would like to hear about your mining experience more than our escapades."

"I'm enjoying both," she said with a smile.

"I have run the Fernandez properties. Two mines produced silver until they closed them down. The ore got so poor they couldn't afford to mill it."

"That's something that could happen to you," Slocum warned Betty.

"I understand," she said, and told Villa to continue.

He went on to talk about his knowledge of timbering and hardrock tunneling. He used his hands all the time to make caverns and T's. The man was a natural flirt too; Slocum knew Pancho couldn't help that. Women from Matamoras to Yuma had been suckered in by his charms. Betty seemed very intent on his explanations.

Then a thought came to Slocum. Those pines would work. He had been sitting there thinking about mine timbers and the cost to buy them and haul them up there when he recalled the trees he had seen on the mesa. They could cut and hew their own. Later he would ride up there and check them out.

The meal completed, Villa and Betty shook hands on the mine deal. Villa left after explaining his plans to get his other wagons ready.

"A very smart man," she said, still seated at the table with Slocum and Meyers.

"He will get the job done," Slocum said.

"Does he have a family in Mexico?" she asked.

"Yes," Slocum said quickly. "He got in some trouble down there with the officials. They are bad in Mexico about collecting bribes. Some officials demanded fifty cents a wagon to inspect the loads of ore he was hauling through their village.

Villa wouldn't pay it, and so he had to come to the States to work.''

"Oh, I see.''

No need to tell her that Villa used a Gatling gun on the officials when they had tried to stop him. She would never understand Mexican policy and how it was being rejected by the people like Villa.

"Can we go back to the ranch?'' she asked with a pleading look.

"I don't know why not. We can go as far as where the road crew will camp today.''

"Good, I can be ready in thirty minutes,'' she said, smiling at him.

"Ernest, stay with her. I'll go get the horses ready at the stables.''

"Is that necessary?'' she asked.

"Yes, there are too many questions unanswered for you not to have a guard.''

"I mean—''

"He's your guard. Go on.''

Meyers nodded, and followed her out of the room ahead of him. Slocum searched the restaurant. That face he had seen the day before—why did it still bother him? There was some connection there. Slocum hadn't seen him since, but his gut instinct told him somehow the man meant trouble.

He left the hotel buttoning his duster as he hurried for the stable. So many things to do. The blast of cold air would be in their faces all day. Maybe the sun would give them some warmth and it would be just a cold blustery day in the desert.

"Put your hands in the air, you're under arrest, Slocum,'' the lawman said behind him.

His arms raised, Slocum turned and saw the face again. The same one he had seen the day before trying to avoid him. Why in the hell was he standing there grinning like a cat as the sheriff opened Slocum's coat and jerked the Colt out of his holster.

"What's the charges?" Slocum wanted to wipe the smug grin off the man's face with his bare fists. He would some day.

"Mr. Moore here swears that you are wanted by the law in Kansas. He has a telegram to prove it. I'm holding you for the Kansas deputy who's en route." The lawman stepped back. "You can put your hands down now. Don't try anything."

So that was the mystery man, the banker Betty had said was such a problem. How did Moore find out about the warrant? No one knew about it—except maybe Milly. But she wouldn't tell his secrets. He needed to get word to Betty. Many things depended on him and they would have to do without him. His arrest couldn't come at a worse time for everyone—except for that smug-acting Moore.

"Can I send a message to Mrs. Wells?"

"There will be time for that later. Get to walking. We're going to the courthouse and lock you up."

"Very well done, Sheriff Meeker," Ralph said as he turned up the fur collar on his expensive coat. He blew his nose in a linen kerchief and then cleared his throat. "I'll be sure that you receive your portion of the reward. I'm off to the telegraph to wire that sheriff that their man is in your custody and for him to send us the reward money."

"They won't pay it," Slocum said.

"Why not?" Moore demanded. Then he sneezed and was forced to blow his nose again.

"The warrant's too old."

"We shall see, gambler." And Moore turned on his heels and left the two of them.

20

"I'll hire a lawyer," Betty said, red-faced, gripping the cell bars with her fists.

"A lawyer won't help. They aren't taking a bond either."

"They've made a mistake," she said.

"Mrs. Wells . . ."

"Betty," she corrected him.

"You and Meyers can go with the crew and be safe. Jones is getting horses for you. Paterson down the street is putting together a herd of cattle for the ranch. Pancho can run the ranch too. You are in good hands. Walt and Joe can keep things in hand. Why don't you go out there? You and Meyers ride out now. Forget me."

"I can't do that." She chewed on her lower lip, and her eyes began to well up with tears. Before she could dry them with a kerchief, the tears streamed down her face.

'You've got to listen," he said, lowering his voice. "I'm not worth crying over. Do what I say." He noticed the deputy was twenty feet away trying to look uninterested. There was no way Slocum could tell her a thing about his plans.

"Here," he said, raising her chin and kissing her with both his cheeks pressed to the cell bars. It was a desperate move, but one that when it was over had told him enough. Somehow he had to get out of his pisspot stinking hellhole and have her.

"Do as I say." He frowned at her.

"Slocum, I will never forget you. Write me?" Her pleading face waiting for his reply.

"I will," he promised, then looked past her for Meyers. "Ernest!"

"Yes," the man said, stepping past the deputy.

"You remember to shoot like you point. Her safety depends on you from now on."

"I will, and I'm sorry. They've made a mistake, haven't they?"

"Take care of her!" he said, ignoring the man's question.

"I will Slocum. I promise," he said as the deputy herded them away.

"Damn, man," a black prisoner said, sitting on his bunk in the next cell. "You sure done got you a fine lady there. My, my, I sure would bend them bars to get out of here and get to her fine body. No disrespect intended."

"None taken," Slocum said as he considered the derringer in his right boot. They'd found the big knife in his other boot, but the small handgun was his key to departing the jail. First he needed the cover of night. He couldn't use the ferry either, or they'd know where he went, so he would need to swim across the cold Gila River if he went back to the Superstitions.

His work in this land wasn't done until that smug Moore was out of the picture. How had he learned about the Kansas warrant? Maybe Milly could answer that for him. He would check with her when he got out.

Ralph stood in Paterson's office. He watched the woman and the drummer mount up at the stables. Without Slocum they would be easy prey. Besides, he was collecting the reward on Slocum as well.

"The deal is all right," the cow trader said, absently going through invoices and brand inspections papers on his desk. Busy with his paperwork, he had no idea what Moore was viewing, nor did he act interested. "She's got the damn money to pay for them cattle. In fact, Able Roderick down at the bank told me she could buy as many cows as I could gather if she wanted them. You know how hard it is to find solid-mouthed cows and them all have a calf beside them?" He paused as if expecting an answer.

"Yes, very hard," Ralph said as he finished wiping his nose. Outside, the two of them were leading a packhorse and heading for the ferry. He breathed a sigh of relief at the knowledge she would soon be out of town and easy prey for him and his men. A sneeze shattered his thoughts, and another depleted the breath in his lungs.

Paterson looked up with the gold reading glasses on the end of his nose. "Getting so I can't find nothing without them."

"What's that?" Moore tried to clear his throat. This illness affecting him was becoming a real handicap to talking, thinking, or doing anything. He blew his nose again into the saturated kerchief.

"My glasses," Paterson said. "I've got to have them to read. Say, an asafetida bag around your neck will help sometimes."

"Smells too bad." Ralph dismissed the notion.

"Eating raw onions can cure them sometimes."

"I'll think on that. When is she coming after her cattle, now that that outlaw who done all her ramrodding is in jail?"

"She's got someone. A Mexican named Villa said he'd have four vaqueros here the day they arrived."

"Who in the hell is he?" More gawdamnn people were meddling in things that didn't concern them.

"Damned if I know. He came in here and started hauling freight and ore."

"Damn Mexicans going to run this country if we don't watch out—" Another hard sneeze broke up his complaint. He mopped up his face and turned toward Paterson.

"Them men of mine show up, send them to the Fronteras house."

"Theresa?" Paterson asked, leaning back in the barrel chair and smiling like he knew her well. "Fine lady—her husband back?"

"No, he's in Mexico." He never came home; she claimed he had a young wife down there to keep him busy.

"Well, ain't that fortunate for you. I mean she's sure nice—fine lady."

"Send those men up to see me when they show up." Had Paterson sampled her wares? Probably sometime back. He looked like a man reliving some bygone pleasantries, like a good toss in horny Theresa's feather bed.

"I will," Paterson said. "You take care of that cold."

Ralph buttoned his coat, turned up the smooth sable collar, and headed into the wind. More than anything he dreaded the outdoor chill he faced. His throat had already become scratchy.

The walk back to Theresa's place was tiring. She immediately noted his condition, and began to treat him with lime juice and a steam kettle with vapors beneath a blanket over his head to better contain the vapors. Too sick to protest, he obeyed her commands and hoped to live through the illness. He chased all her potions with rye whiskey, and soon didn't give a damn.

She undressed him and tucked him into bed under piles of covers, and the sweat began to roll from his pores. She treated his hacking cough with a spoon of a mixture containing lemon, honey, and his whiskey in equal parts. He soon slept in a puddle of his own perspiration—dead to the world.

He awoke once and through bleary eyes saw her seated under a shawl on a chair beside a small candle on the table.

"What time is it?" he asked, groggy with sleep and the cold.

"Seven o'clock," she said rearranging the covers around his face.

"My boys?"

"No one has come," she said.

He fell back deep asleep.

"You ever been to Goldfield?" Moses Teafeau asked, making conversation.

"A few times," Slocum said.

"You a gambler, huh?"

"I do some. Why? Did you see me there sometime?"

"No, sah, I never seen you before that turnkey brung you in here. But yesterday, they come in here saying that someone done cut some whore by the name of Milly's throat in Goldfield."

"You serious? Have they got the killer?" Slocum blinked at the man.

"Well, I figured they'd brung you in for doing it."

"No, she was a friend of mine. You hear anything else? Anything. Tell me. I need to find her murderer."

"They don't have any leads."

"I do!" Slocum snarled. Moore was the one that she'd warned him about. Somehow the banker was involved in her death, and he had to learn more about the man to ever prove it.

"You know who killed her?" Moses frowned at him in disbelief.

"I know who probably did it."

"But you in jail. How you going to prove anything?"

"What are you in for?"

"Eating beef didn't belong to me."

"Whose was it?"

"I ain't sure."

"Keep your mouth shut," Slocum said under his breath. "We may be getting paroled sooner than you think."

"I be ready."

"Get that jailer in here." Slocum showed him the derringer in his palm.

"Oh, turnkey, I done been poisoned on your damn sorry food!" The man began to wail and hug his stomach. "Do something! Come quick! I be needing a doctor!" He dropped on to his side on the floor like a colicky horse, kicking spasmodically, and then curled into a ball.

"What the hell's wrong with you, nigger?" the guard demanded at the black man's cell door. "Get your ass up off that floor."

"I can't," Moses gasped, holding his stomach in pain.

"I'll kick some damn sense in you." The deputy turned the key with a great click as Slocum stood looking on at the next cell. In two steps, he stomped inside and began swinging his boot toe into Moses' leg.

"That's enough!" Slocum ordered, and the deputy whirled.

The pupils of his eyes widened at the sight of a two-barrel derringer pointed at his heart. His hands went skyward and Moses jerked the keys away from him. A clamor from the other prisoners started through the cells.

"Hush!" Moses ordered. "Next man yells out is dead." He had the deputy's handgun in his fist. "We all getting out, but there's two more out front we got to silence." He tossed the keys to Slocum, who caught them with a sigh of relief.

"He got cuffs on him?" he asked Moses as he undid his own cell door.

"Yes."

"Cuff him, then put him on his belly on your bunk. Gag him good."

"What about us?" another prisoner demanded.

"You're coming out after we get the other two guards. Be quiet till then." He slipped toward the entrance, hoping no one had heard the uproar.

The entrance door led to the sheriff's office. He could see it by peering carefully through the small window. Two men were in there. One was working on papers, the other making coffee.

"What next?" Moses joined him out of breath.

"Don't kill them," Slocum whispered. "We don't need anyone hurt if we can help it."

"I savvy. A gunshot brings us trouble."

"Right."

"Go."

"Stand and deliver!" Slocum shouted as he slammed the door open, and the deputy making coffee let the pot clang to the floor in his rush to obey. The one at the desk whirled, looking for a minute like he was considering trying something.

"You won't get away with this!" said the lawman sitting in the chair.

"Sorry, gents, we have found all your prisoners innocent and we're letting them wing away." He carefully checked the pair for any weapons, and then cuffed them behind their backs and marched them into a cell. When that cell was locked, the manacled and gagged lawmen glared at him. He tossed the keys to the next prisoner with outstretched hands. The man caught it with a shout of joy.

"Be quiet," Slocum cautioned them. "Come on, Moses. We've got ground to cover to get to Mexico."

"Yes, we sure do."

Slocum found his coat in the sheriff's closet. They battered apart the chain on the gun rack, and each took a rifle and a pocket full of shells as the other inmates spilled into the outer room.

He and Moses hurried from the sheriff's office. He led the way down the back stairs, two at a time. Maybe the chaos of releasing the others would mask their escape. He hoped so. When they reached the rear door, they checked outside, and then ran across the courtyard for the businesses across the street.

"I hate to steal a horse," Slocum said in the alley, trying to catch his breath. "But we need transportation."

"There's two right there." Moses indicated with a thumb over his shoulder.

"Get one. I'll get the other."

"Good. Which way we really going?"

"East."

"Ain't that Apache land?" Moses asked as they ran.

"I ain't wanted by them."

"Me neither. Let's go," Moses said. In a rush, they untied the reins, ducked under the rack, and mounted the cow ponies like cats. They were gone before their owners were ever the wiser.

Jumping an irrigation ditch on their flight from town, Slocum realized for the first time the cold night wind was sweeping in his face. Encouraged by the sharp slap of the reins to their rumps, the ponies made the leap across the water. The men rode parallel to the ditch for several miles, then turned and headed out through the low greasewood for the distant outline of mountains.

Somewhere out there, Dirty Shirt Jones was gathering horses among the Apaches. They would need some fresh ones by the time they found him, and then he could return their borrowed ones to their owners. Making their mounts trot, they headed into the inky darkness with only the glow of stars to see by. Slocum wanted miles between them and the courthouse jail.

Somewhere a mournful coyote yipped and then howled. And Slocum bobbed his head in agreement. *Yes, like you, brother dog, we too are lost in the night, hunted and scorned by righteous folks.*

21

"Some outlaws have broke out of the jail, and they turned all the lunatics loose. Why, they're running over town," Theresa shouted, coming through the back door with her arms full of the fresh fruit and items she'd bought to treat his cold. "Sheriff Meeker is deputizing men to ride in a posse!"

From under a blanket, with steam boiling from the spout into his face, Ralph raised his head up and through his rheumy eyes tried to focus on her. What the hell did she mean that some outlaws broke out of jail?

"Don't tell me Slocum got out of jail?" he asked in disbelief.

"They're all out, including every one of those lunatics. Did you know that crazy Markus Brown was running around town naked all morning until they finally caught him." She shook her head in disgust as she unloaded the fresh lemons and limes on the table. "They can't punish those outlaws enough for doing that."

"Why's that?" He frowned at her. Who did that hurt? She made less sense than a lunatic herself. How in the devil had Slocum escaped the jail?

"They should have sent that demented old man to the insane asylum by now. Do you think those poor virgins should have to look at that hairy devil running all over Main Street with his pecker flopping around?''

"They don't have to look. How did they get out?" He frowned at her. His mind was so numbed with his affliction he couldn't even think.

"How should I know—wait, someone smuggled a six-gun to a black man, I think."

"That black man may cost me four hundred dollars," he said, trying to stand.

"Who was he?" she asked.

"How the hell should I know! Slocum is the pain of my days, and now the sumbitch is out of the jail! Gawdamn, tell me what else is going wrong?"

He broke off into a fit of coughing that doubled him over, each gasp rasping his throat like pain-filled stabs of lightning. Trying to steady himself on the table, he grew weaker and weaker.

"We need to buy some food," Slocum said in Spanish to the older Apache woman they met on the trail. The noon sun was high when they rode up to her.

Her dark eyes like those of a hawk, she examined them with her head drawn back, using her hand against the sun's glare. She did not act afraid of them. Considering the offer, she did not speak for some time.

"You rode with Wolf Tail," she said sharply.

"Yes," Slocum said.

"Come." She hugged together the shawl on her shoulders and then nodded. Turning in her tracks, she started back on the gravel path. They booted their horses to follow the old woman up the winding canyon choked with mesquites.

"What we using for money?" Moses whispered.

"We have plenty of money." Slocum reached in his coat

pocket and began to drop cartridges from one hand to the other to demonstrate his wealth of bullets.

"She going to feed us or eat us?" Moses asked through his teeth.

"She's Wolf Tail's squaw."

"You know her?"

"No, but she knows me from when I campaigned with her husband."

She stopped and looked hard at Moses. "Him buffalo soldier?" she finally asked in Spanish.

Slocum shrugged. "I'm not sure." Whether it was good or bad, she continued up the sandy wash bed until he saw on the slopes the cluster of wickiups that were covered with scraps of canvas and blankets. A few small cur dogs barked; several women and men came outside to see who had invaded their place. Naked children stopped their play to stand on the arroyo bank and stare down at the black and white men in their midst.

"Sit here, no one will bother you. You are my guest," she announced, and Slocum thanked her, anxious to stand and stretch his legs. They had ridden a great distance since the night before.

"You don't speak Apache?" Moses asked, looking around suspiciously.

"Not good enough. Spanish is pretty universal among them."

"I savvy enough Mexican to get by. But I can't say my skin don't crawl out here worse than it did in that old jail."

"In the long run it beats Yuma prison."

"You been there?"

"Trust me, I'll take my chances with the Apaches over that."

"Where you going from here?" Moses asked, loosening his cinch to allow his pony to rest.

"We get those horses from Jones, I have to swing back and

make some things go right for that woman. That means fixing a certain banker's plow.''

''You don't mind me trailing along?'' he asked with a side-long glance.

''I can get an Apache boy to take you through their land and point out New Mexico to you on the far side.'' He wanted to give the man a chance to get clear of the country. If he didn't take it, fine, but still he wanted Moses to know he could ride on to a safe place, or at least a different one.

''I still would like to help you.''

''You might be taking a big chance staying around here.''

''Nothing to lose.'' He shrugged as if to dismiss any concern.

''Moses.'' Slocum extended his hand to the man. ''Welcome to trouble. Here comes our food.''

The squaw came carrying two pottery vessels. Steam rose from them as she grew closer. Slocum wondered what the mixture was made from, but decided his hollow belly could stand anything called food.

She handed each of them a pot. He thanked her after taking his, and offered her brass cartridges, but she declined them, mumbling something in Apache he could not understand.

With bone spoons, they dug into the spicy mixture of chiles and stringy meat. Probably horse, he decided. They sat on a chair-high rock and nodded in appreciation for her tasty food. The braver onlookers drew closer. Naked children, their skin dusty from play, lined up to peer at the intruders. Boys and girls alike stood in the line, their exposed genders obvious. Many held small bows and arrows like the ones they would use as grown-ups to hunt and to kill.

''They haven't seen many black men,'' Slocum said casually to his new partner.

''You tell them I ain't never seen this many Apaches.'' Then Moses laughed aloud between spoons of the food.

"Does it rub off?" an older boy asked in Spanish, looking with interest at the black man.

"No. Him *oso negro*," Slocum said with a thumb tossed towards Moses.

"What's that mean?" he asked under his breath.

"They wondered if you fell into a tar pot. I told them you were a black bear."

"That's good?"

"Yes, they don't eat bears."

"Good, me *oso negro*," he said louder, and the children began to laugh. Soon the two men joined them in their laughter. Finished with their meal, they handed the bowls and spoons back to the woman, thanking her.

She had not seen Jones, nor had she heard of his horse-buying. They had to ride on, and Slocum hoped they didn't miss him. The pair mounted up and rode east into the hills. Somewhere Dirty Shirt Jones was plying his business—they needed to locate him.

22

His head stuffed from his cold, Moore had sent Theresa to the livery to get his sorrel horse. There'd been no sign of his men at Paterson's. Obviously they had ridden back to the ranch, and had not gone through Goldfield when they didn't find the woman at her ranch. So they were waiting for him at the hideout. He needed to stop this road building, and all before this Villa got up there and hauled some of that rich ore to the smelter. Sick or not, he had to. He blew his nose and shook his head.

Why couldn't he think? This stinking cold had his mind bogged. Theresa had offered to ride with him, but she didn't need to know about his business. Somehow he would make it. The steam and lemons helped some, but his nose was still stuffed, and he'd coughed until his scrotum hurt.

"You are crazy to make such a ride," she said after coming back, steadying him onto the horse. "See, you are weak as a baby. You will fall off and die out there." She stepped back and shook her head in disapproval. "Go kill yourself! This is stupid."

He drew in a ragged breath and gripped the saddlehorn in his right hand. There was no way to explain what he must do—he shook his head and dismissed her concern. He booted the horse and started for the ferry.

"I will pray for your stupid life!" she screamed after him.

"Pray then, dammit!" he thought. "I can't help it. I should have already killed the stupid woman who's about to ruin my life." He forced the sorrel into a trot, and the pain of the gait threatened to break him into pieces; still, he made the horse keep going. He had to find Gates and the others. They had to—He shut his eyes against the bright sun and tried to stop the deep cough from coming. He couldn't.

"You sure look peaked today," the ferryman said as he led the horse onto the deck of the boat.

"I feel that way too, Tom," Moore said. He wanted to lie down in the bright sun out of the wind and sleep forever. Still, he lacked a long distance of being where he needed to be.

Across the Gila on the north bank, he departed the barge, then with effort, he mounted up again and began to trot the horse. It would be past dark when he got to the cabin. If he could keep his eyes open that long. Time and again, he found himself dropping off to sleep and ready to fall out of the saddle. Unable to shake the drowsiness, he finally roped himself in with the lariat. The arrangement was not all that good, but at least he might wake up before he was completely unseated. It was the best he could hope for under the conditions.

His vision swarmed and his head swirled with waves of dizziness. Then he began to sweat and wanted to shed all his clothing, but he knew that was only the fever making him think crazily. Perhaps if he walked beside the horse? No, then he might not be able to remount. Once he found the men, then he could go on to his house in Picket Post. Maybe Doc Slade could find a remedy for his cold. Hell, that Mexican witch Theresa didn't know anything but how to lie on her back and please men.

He reached in the saddlebag, remembering her cough medicine, and took a deep swig from the bottle. She had filled the brown bottle with a mixture of whiskey, honey, and lemon. The liquor warmed him going down and settled his coughing. In a short while he felt good enough to lope the horse. Then the ropes he had lashed himself in with began to bind him and he was forced to undo them.

Long past dark, he wound up the canyon seeing the light on in the shack. They were there. His eyes by then were so heavy he couldn't keep them open to see. He dropped heavily from the saddle at the front stoop.

"That you, Boss?" Gates asked from the doorway.

"Hell, no—" His reply was cut off by more raucous coughing, until he thought he would piss in his pants.

"You sick?"

"No—I'm pretending." He shrugged off the man's hands and rushed into the shack.

Through his drooping eyelids he could see the surly dogs he had hired, sitting around with their hands full of playing cards and roll-your-own cigarettes dangling from their lips. The smoke was thick enough to cut with a knife.

"Come morning." He rested his hands on the table for support. "I want you to ride up there and kill ever sumbitch working on that road to the mine and the woman too."

"They ain't up there," Gates protested.

"They went back yesterday."

"Dammit, we spent two nights at that ranch waiting on them."

"I don't—" The exertion had brought up more crud in his throat, and he coughed on it until his breath ran out. "I don't care what you waited—they sent a crew up there to build a damn road to that mine and she took a train of burros loaded with supplies to the ranch."

"We'll stop them, won't we, boys?" Gates pounded his fist on the table.

The bob of heads around the table hardly reassured Moore. He'd done all he could, ridden forty miles sicker than a horse. Even if there were bedbugs and lice in them, he was going to lie down and sleep in one of those bunks. He didn't give a damn—he was too tired to go another foot.

"Where can I sleep?"

"Oh, take my bunk," Gates offered.

"Which one?" he asked, and then blew his nose again in the wet kerchief.

"That one. Need any help?"

"No. I just need to sleep some of this off." Then he sneezed violently—this had to stop sometime. But when? He crawled in under the covers on the lumpy mattress, jerked his hat off, and laid his head down, pulling blankets over him. She had to be stopped from opening that mine somehow—that was all he knew.

Slocum and Moses spent a cold night without blankets, feeding a small fire in the wash bed. They had talked to several Apaches during the past day, but none had seen Jones, nor had they heard of his horse-buying activities. Slocum was beginning to think that in another day's ride they would be to Fort Apache and still have no sign of him.

He had dozed some, until he heard riders coming in the predawn. On his feet, he loosened the Colt in his holster, and Moses joined him.

"What's coming?"

"I'm not certain, but Apaches don't do big business at night. They are afraid their spirits will have to stay in the dark forever if they get killed."

"Hey, Slocum!"

"It's Jones," he said, holstering his gun as the slew-footed gray and the outline of the big man came into view.

"You looking for me?" Jones dropped heavily from the horse with a ring of his spur rowels. The string of horses he had led snorted, grateful to be stopped, and stomped about as he tied the lead to his saddlehorn.

"Been all over looking for you," Slocum said as the man joined him and Moses.

"I only had a dozen horses bought when a boy came and said a white man and a black man were on the reservation looking for me."

"Jones, meet Moses." The two men shook hands. "That banker Moore had me detained in the county hoosegow. Moses here and me liberated ourselves. We need you to take these horses back because we borrowed them from some cowboys. Then we need a couple new horses and saddles."

"Where did the woman go?" Jones asked.

"To the Superstitions with Ernest, the scouts, and Villa's men."

"Good. Joe and Walter will see to her safety. No blankets?" He looked around.

"No. See, me and Moses are tough," Slocum said, rubbing his sleeves briskly for warmth.

"Get your horses. Mary Two Hearts has some blankets at her store, and she'll have some food too. She's probably got some saddles for sale. Her place is only a few hours from here."

"We're coming," Slocum said.

"Amen," Moses said, scraping dirt on top of the fire with the side of his sole. "I was in a storm once with only a yellow slicker, and if I'd had two of them things to wear I'd sure froze to death. But man, it has got colder than that up here since sundown."

•   •   •

The store of Mary Two Hearts was built of small pine logs and nestled under a grove of fresh-leaved cottonwoods. The sod planted on the roof had begun to green. Everyone dismounted, and Jones put his horses in the corral. The others hitched theirs to the rack, and then Jones joined them.

"Hey," Jones shouted to the tall woman who came to the door. Dressed in a deerskin dress that hugged her ripe figure, she rushed into his arms, and despite her size, he easily swung her around in a circle with her Apache boots off the ground.

"Good to see you!" she said as he set her down. She slapped him on the chest with a palm that would have staggered the ordinary man. Her smile widened as she looked over Moses and Slocum.

"My friends need to buy two saddles, blankets, and some food," Jones said.

Her dark eyes met Slocum's. They held the glance for a moment as she caught her breath. Slocum watched her bust line rise and fall under the leather fringe and beaded work. He felt certain her subtle body would entertain a man.

"You come in," she said, and waved for them to follow her inside.

She dragged out two older saddles from her stock that looked good enough to use. Slocum and Moses inspected the cinches and the latigoes to be certain they would hold, and agreed with a nod that they would serve their needs.

"How much?" Slocum asked.

"They are good. Twenty dollars for both. I'll throw in the bridles and some pads."

"Fair enough," Slocum said, not anxious to argue with her.

"I'll toss it on a horse for you. Which one you want?" Moses asked, motioning toward the outside as he gathered them up.

"Either," Slocum said.

"You comin'?" Moses asked now.

"I'll be along in a minute," Slocum assured him. "Jones, pay the lady, seems my money was removed in Florence."

The big man grinned and dug out two ten-dollar gold pieces. "He still needs a couple blankets"

"They aren't free," she said sharply.

"He can pay for them," Slocum said to assure her.

From the shelf she took down two new-looking wool ones. "Ten dollars."

"You have had them for months," Jones argued.

She started to put them back when Slocum caught her arm and shook his head. They needed them and had little time for Jones's dickering.

"Pay her," Slocum said, looking deep into the brown pools of her eyes. He still held her by the upper arm, and his gaze did not flicker, nor did hers.

"He is looking after our boss's money. Forgive him, will you?" he asked with a smile for her.

"Hmm," she snorted through her long slender nose. "You should come again by this place."

"Maybe I shall."

"I dare you to," she said as if no one else was in the room and Jones was miles away.

"Nice to meet you, Mary Two Hearts," Slocum said softly.

She nodded, and then he released her arm.

"Get your own blankets," Jones said, and broke for the door.

Slocum used the last moments to smile at her before she turned away looking embarrassed. His arms full of the soft woolen Pentletons, he spun on his boot heels and headed for the horses. His stomach turned over at the thought that he was leaving such a fine example of ripe womanhood—he would have to come back and see her.

23

Still, in a fog, Ralph awoke before dawn. The snoring in the room was loud as he fought his way to the front door and then relieved his bladder off the front porch. The cooler air made him shiver as he finished and then paused to blow his nose. He was no better than he had been. They had no time to waste and needed to get going.

"Get out of bed. We've got things to do!" he shouted from the door. They needed to be in the saddle and gone.

He ignored the groans and grumbling of the men. They could like it or lump it, he didn't give a damn. If they didn't stop that bitch from reopening the mine, he was sunk and would have to flee the territory, and that would mean they all lost their jobs. He wouldn't be taking the likes of them with him—he would be traveling light, making fast tracks.

Maybe he'd go to Denver; it was bustling and there should be some large opportunities there. But if he managed to stop her and take over the mine, he could stay in the territory as long as he wanted. He might even get into politics—there should be some real money to be made in government. Contacts and opportunities were where the dollars rose like cream in milk.

One of the breeds was rustling up the fire in the stove, and another was pouring water from a bucket into the coffeepot. Ralph dropped on the bunk and scrubbed his beard-stubbled face in his palms. Another day like the last one and it was liable to kill him. Still, without him to oversee it all, they would probably screw up and let her get away.

Where in hell was Slocum? Had that two-bit gambler run when he'd broken out? There was a chance he would turn up with the Wells woman. Good, they'd kill him when they went after her and *he* would collect the reward.

Finally, after a greasy breakfast of potatoes and deep-fried slices of a deer haunch, they mounted up and headed for the north and the Superstitions. It would probably take them all day to get there, but by dark they could sneak up and finish off the road crew.

Taking a place in the rear of the line, Moore tried to keep from coughing up his guts. He swigged on what was left of Theresa's remedy to control it. Several times he saw one or two of the men look back at him as if he might die at any minute, but he didn't, and he had no plans for dying either. They could go to hell—when he finally owned the Iron Mountain Mine he'd cut them some slack.

If he could only get over this damn depleting cold. He booted the sorrel. Best damn horse in the territory. They stopped at a stream flowing with the spring rains and watered their horses at mid-morning. The men rolled cigarettes and sat about cross-legged to smoke while he tried to blow the congestion from his head.

It was no use, and his chest had become so tight that even breathing hurt. He sat on the grass and wondered if he would ever be well. Damn cold anyway.

"You able to ride?" Gates asked.

"Gawdamnit, yes," he swore, and forced himself to remount. The exertion weakened him further, but he managed to get into the saddle and despite nearly blacking out, managed to push his horse forward after them. They'd have to get tougher to leave him. His hands clasped the saddlehorn in a death grip.

By late afternoon, they were close to Iron Mountain, and Gates sent Two Feathers to scout the road builders' camp. Meanwhile, they made a small fire to boil coffee. With the wind out of the west, Gates assured Moore that her bunch on the mountain couldn't smell their smoke. He also issued some pepper fiery jerky that threatened to break Moore's teeth. Wrapped in a couple of blankets, Moore sat shivering on his butt and not giving a damn—except for the fact that they could soon finish this business and kill her.

He imagined killing her slowly—perhaps like that red-headed whore in Goldfield. Press her face down with his knee in her back, and then draw her head back with a handful of her hair—Coughing cut off his thoughts.

She was the very reason he had this deadly cold. Why, he never got sick working in the bank. That dirty bitch and her papers had come swirling into his office and turned his entire life upside down. Now he bent over in convulsive coughs, trying to extract more green phlegm from his throat. His back arched forward as he coughed until his breath grew exhausted and he grew faint.

He'd kill her!

"Gawdamn Apaches!" someone shouted, and Moore looked around through his bleary eyes. There were shots. His eyes weren't focusing. His hand went for his gun butt; four screaming bucks swept through camp in a rush taking all of their horses, including his good sorrel.

He rose to his feet in a rage and emptied his Colt at the fleeting figures. There were shots all around. Those red bastards were taking his sorrel and he couldn't stop them. Those stinking damn blanket-asses had kept him from the mine up until now. On top of that, they'd taken his good horse.

Where had they come from? He looked around. The two breeds' rifles were still smoking, and both of Gates's handguns were doing the same. Carlos, the Mexican, was down, and Gates rushed to see about him, holstering his pistols.

Not a sign. The Apaches were gone like smoke. Moore turned an ear to listen, but heard nothing. His head was so stopped up he couldn't hear thunder, he decided, as he forced himself to join the others standing around the Mexican's prone body.

"He's dead," Gates said, raising up and shaking his head warily. The bullet wounds in Carlos's chest seeped blood; the black hole under his blank left eye was dry.

"Have we got a single horse left?" Ralph asked, not seeing one as he looked about. The Apaches had made a clean sweep of their stock.

"Hell, no, we better start back," Gates said. "We can't do nothing without horses."

"Go back on what, our boot soles?" Ralph shouted.

"Ain't my fault, them red bastards was that close."

"Won't Two Feathers come back?" he asked, not wanting to argue with the stupid man.

"Sure."

"Then we can wait for him. He can go back and get us some horses."

"This ain't no young-buck business," Lafferty grumbled.

"What's he talking about?" Ralph asked, busy trying to study the side of Iron Mountain that he could see from their location. The sun was setting and the slopes were bathed in a purple shadow.

"They heard that Natise is off the reservation," Gates explained. "They think he sent them boys to steal our horses."

"So?" Ralph asked, still not impressed.

"Maybe you don't mind to die. We do," the breed Coy said.

"Where in the hell are you going?" Gates asked as the two breeds started off headed south.

"We won't stay with him around."

"Son of a bitch. What next?" Ralph demanded in Gates's face.

"I ain't liking it either, but I won't quit you."

"Let them go," Ralph said in disgust, and waved them away with his back to them. "They drew wages when it was easy. Gets a little tough and they go yellow."

There was no help, and they were a good thirty miles from town. What else would happen? Those red niggers had taken his best horse before he could even draw his gun. When he got his hands on that woman, he'd strangle the life out of her with his bare hands.

Moses and Slocum had pushed their fresh horses hard. They'd forded the Gila and were headed into the foothills when Slocum spotted the dust. He indicated to Moses that they should take the wash; reining to a walk, they rode side by side up the narrow side canyon.

"What's wrong?" Moses asked as he dismounted, taking his rifle from the scabbard.

"Someone is moving east. I saw their dust."

"Who?" the black man asked, taking the reins to Slocum's bay.

"I'm not sure. I'm going to climb up there and see who it is." He indicated the cholla-clad slope that rose above them.

"I'll hold the horses," Moses said.

"Good, I'll be back. No need to ride into a trap."

"That's for sure."

Despite his slick leather boot soles, Slocum managed a half run up the steep face. He worked his way around rock outcroppings, dodging greasewood, prickly pear beds, and the pale jointed cholla until he dropped carefully on the ground at the ridge, his rifle beside him. From his position, he could view the wide valley between himself and the back side of the Superstitions.

The source of the dust was obvious; he could make out several squaws leading loaded horses with their children on top of the packs. A moving party meant their men were somewhere else. Was Betty safe? Who was off the reservation? Renegades usually went to Mexico when they left San Carlos—what were they doing up there? Had he sent Betty into a nest of them?

He rubbed his sweaty palms on his britches and picked up his rifle. Frowning in thought, he planned their next moves; they needed to cross that valley and be certain that Betty and her bunch were safe. He looked to the west to check the sun; they had a couple hours of daylight left. Betty and the crew were across that valley and on the mountain, and there was no way to hide his and Moses' route if the Apaches were watching them.

He regretted sending Jones to Florence to return the horses and saddles they'd borrowed. The big man could have figured out some diversion. At the moment, he needed a way to fool the Apaches, but his mind could think of nothing but a death ride for perhaps three miles of open country. Then, if they were too late and the whole bunch had been wiped out—no, the Apaches couldn't take down that large a party.

Still, desperate as the renegades must be, they would have little reservation about killing whites for their possessions. Besides, Betty and the others had enough supplies to get a large band of Apaches to safety in the Sierra Madres. Placing his feet carefully, he hurried off the hillside.

"Who's out there?" Moses asked.

"Apache women and plenty of them."

"What you got in mind?" Moses looked taken back by the news, and looked around nervously.

"Make a run for the mountain."

"In the daylight?" Moses squinted his left eye at him.

"Yes. If my friends need help, then we better get to them."

"That gal, she's over the other side of them Injuns?"

"Right. You can turn right here and go your way. This ain't your fight."

"Reckon I just made it that way," Moses said, swinging on his horse. Then he drew his Colt and ran the cylinder down his sleeve to check the loads. Lowering the hammer, he re-holstered it. "Which way we going out of here?"

"This way. I call it whip and ride," Slocum said with a grin.

24

Ralph shivered holding his arms as he stalked back and fort
under his blanket cape. The temperature must be below freez-
ing. Between the damn coughing and blowing his sore nose
he felt whipped. The two worthless breeds had walked off—
he hoped the damn Apaches got them. More than likely the
would lead those bloody butchers back. If he ever got
chance, he'd kill both Lafferty and Coy. Why, they'd draw
his pay for months. Kill them was what he'd do to them—n
good bastards.

In the pearl starlight, he could make out Gates snoring o
his back, all curled up on the ground in a thin wrapper. He
he must have a stove inside him to not freeze to death. H
own face was burning up, and inside he had icicles in h
veins. Why did he have to have a bad cold at a time like this
How much longer until dawn?

He resumed pacing across the camp. This whole thing ha
become impossible. How much time did he have left? Ho
long before they sent another auditor from the banking com
mission—hired a new one to take Johnstone's place. Mayb
until mid-summer, at the latest in the winter. With luck, Ralp
could have the mine operating in six months, with enough o

nined and shipped—but damn, he needed close to twenty
housand. It was too much money to ever hope for. Maybe he
should cut his losses and run. All his hard work in this place,
all his hours of scheming and planning, would be burned out
ike a falling star without a trace.

Dawn finally came. He built up the fire and warmed his
hands over the flames, but the smoke aggravated his cough.
Spitting up strings of phlegm, he looked up at the rider coming
up the dry wash.

"Wake up, Gates! He's got her!" He could hardly believe
his eyes as he stepped back in awe. There before him came
he haggard-looking Wells woman riding in front of Two
Feathers. They sat double on his horse when the Indian
topped before him.

"This is the squaw you want?" the buck asked, slipping
rom behind and jerking her down.

"Yes! Thank God, you've got her."

"Damn you, Moore! You won't get by with this!" she said,
truggling with his hold on her arm and recovering her bal-
nce.

"My, Mrs. Wells, when we get through with you, you'll be
egging, not threatening us." Then he stood with his arms
olded and nodded in approval, filled with power and strength.
Iow much better could it be? "Yes, you have done very good,
wo Feathers." Then he broke into a fit of choking.

"Let go of me, you filthy scum." She struggled with Two
eathers, who ignored her and bound her hands with a leather
ong.

Recovered from his fit of coughing, Ralph mopped his
outh and perspiring face. Things weren't lost. He had the
ey to everything in his grasp.

"Damn, you got her," Gates said, walking around her, in-
ecting her.

Two Feathers squatted on his haunches and smoked a cig arette. "Where are the others?"

"Apaches stole our horses last night. Sons a bitches came in here and shot Carlos dead over there and them two breed run off like jackrabbits," Gates said in disgust.

"Go get fresh horses," Two Feathers said, and in a boun was on his horse. "Be back by dark."

Ralph looked at Gates. Would the Indian come back? The had no one else to trust—they did have her, though. H watched Two Feathers ride over the rise and disappear int the sea of greasewood.

"He'll be back. He won't want to miss rutting her," Gate said with a knowing smile and a nod toward Betty.

"You won't get away with this," she said.

"You ain't got a thing to say about it. You better shut you mouth before I slap it shut," Ralph said, taking a threatenin step toward her.

"My men will be coming after you—"

His backhand swing slammed her head sideways. Then h caught her upper arm and jerked her close to his mouth wit a vise-like grip. Coughing and unable to talk, he managed t glare coldly enough to silence her.

"The game's over. Slocum's run off," he finally manage "That derby-hat runt ain't going to save no one, and the damn Mexicans up there are scared of their own shadows."

"You'll see," she said, leaning as far as possible away fro him.

"Yes, I will see." He shoved her to the ground. "Sta there." He whipped out his wrinkled kerchief and blew h nose. The damn cold would be the ruin of him yet. He sa her burning eyes following him. Well, she was as good signed on the deed.

She might be a little tougher than that redheaded whor Still, he'd break her will. There wasn't a woman alive l couldn't wring obedience out of. If he had to, he'd forge her signature. The mine was as good as his, if they could manage to get out of there. With her dead, there would be nothing to stop him.

"Gates, get up and go be sure no one followed him."

"Sure, sure. I was making some coffee, we got the fixings and all."

"I'll do it. I don't want to be snuck up on. Damn, I have to think of everything." He shook his head and looked over to where she sat on the ground. He couldn't afford to lose her—not after all this.

Brittle greasewood whipped their stirrups as they drove their mounts across the desert floor. The horses that Jones had bought were well bred, and no doubt had once been the property of ranchers, for their stride was long and sure, even in the rough footing. Spread out twenty feet apart, he and Moses used their mounts in a full race, screaming like banshees at the top of their lungs.

At their approach, some of the Apache women began to panic and went to whipping their mounts. Others headed for washes to hide in as the two split through the dispersed band. Slocum hated to panic innocents, but his plans were to rout the women and try to draw the men away from Betty's camp.

Past the party, they crossed a deep dry wash, scrambled up the far side, and reached the high ground. On the bank, Slocum checked his hard-breathing horse and looked back. Satisfied there was no one on their back trail, he let his horse settle into a gallop. He hoped to conserve the animal's strength; they still had the mountain to climb. More than anything else, he needed to keep his wits and his eyes peeled for trouble, but they passed the last mile to the base of the mountain without incident.

Reining in their blowing horses, he shared a hard smile with

Moses. Both men were recovering from the past tense moments. If one of their horses had fallen, or if there had been some bucks close by, they might not now be starting up the trail. Slocum drew a deep breath in relief, and followed Moses' horse up the sheer pathway.

"This the way to heaven?" Moses asked.

"It is more earthly than that," Slocum promised.

"I'll be glad to be there."

"So will I." Slocum looked skyward and wondered how the crew was doing. In another half hour, he'd know. He reined the bay around the sharp turns and wondered how the spooked Indian women were doing. Where were their men? That bothered him more than anything. Of course, he knew an Apache woman could disappear in the desert. A band that large had once left even Crook wondering where they went. And only an Apache scout could find them, teasing his white counterparts the whole time he tracked them down. Apaches were uncanny at dogging their own kind—the Army never would have found any of that band without the Apache scout.

"Someone's coming down," Moses said over his shoulder.

Slocum rose in the stirrups. It was Ernest Meyers on his gray pony. What was wrong for him to be coming?

"Let me by," Slocum said as they came to where the trail flattened. He nudged the bay past Moses' and up the mountain.

"Thank God!" Ernest shouted. "I recognized your hat. The Apaches have taken Betty. I did all I could, but no one can find a track."

"Damn, when did they get her?"

"An hour ago. She went to relieve herself and she never came back." Meyers shook his head in defeat. "What'll we do?"

Slocum looked across the mountains to the west; the sun would soon set. The Apaches had taken her. He closed his eyes at the thought of her being in their hands. Damn, they had no respect—a white woman was little more than chattel. A man they killed. A woman they used. Maybe he could find Natise and offer himself in her place. Where was the chief at?

"Let's talk to Walt and Joe." Slocum pointed to the top and let Meyers rein his pony around to lead the way. "They may have a clue."

"They couldn't find a single track. Said it was sure enough an Injun took her." Meyers whipped his mount into cat-hopping up the trail.

"What next?" Moses asked.

"We've got to find her," Slocum said, and sent his horse after the little man.

He gazed across the desert floor far below that was fast filling in with the shadows of evening as the sun's orange rays bathed them from aloft in their final quest on Iron Mountain. Where was Jones at? He would be there in another twelve hours if he had no delays. He was the only one good enough to track her kidnappers. *Betty, we're coming, stay alive, girl.*

25

"Someone's coming." Ralph rose to his feet at the sound of hoofbeats. It was past noon; he had not expected Two Feathers to be back so soon. But thank God, the bareheaded Indian was coming in leading a string of horses. Gates came back running on his boot heels.

"He's bringing horses."

"I can see that he is. Get up, woman, we're getting the hell out of here," he said, pulling Betty to her feet.

"Let go of me." She tried to jerk free of his grasp.

"Listen, you either straighten up or else I'll slap some sense into you." He pulled her roughly close to his face. "I'm going to enjoy watching you crawl."

"Anyone crawls it will be you," she said defiantly.

"We'll see. Get aboard that horse or you'll go belly-down." He shoved her in the direction of the horse. "Good work, Two Feathers," he said as the horses blew from the hard run. "Let's go to the hideout."

The buck grinned and nodded that he had heard. Two Feathers held the reins to her mount as his horse twisted impatiently and stomped to be going. Satisfied she couldn't escape, Ralph took the reins of his mount from Gates and swung up. The

162

horse bolted, and he barely contained him with the bit. The horse was acting as if he might buck any minute, and Ralph closed his free hand on the saddlehorn and checked him. Damn Apaches had his best horse and he had drawn a half-broncy one. All his attention focused on the animal between his legs, and he finally was forced to boot him after the others who were galloping away from him.

After two halfhearted bucks, his mount finally broke into a lope. The notion that the horse might pile him into a bed of cactus made Ralph's stomach roll over. A bitter sour taste rose in his throat as the stiff-legged animal raced to catch the others. All he needed was to be thrown—damn, what was going to happen to him next?

He looked back over his shoulder for any pursuit. Nothing behind him. They could never track them on the hard ground. When this was over, he must reward that buck for kidnapping her. It was worth every dollar he'd paid all of them. His future would be secure once the new deed was recorded. There was no way to connect him to her disappearance. He smiled, then was caught in a fit of coughing.

She'd pay for all his troubles. When he got through with her, the other two could have her. That would teach her. When they finished, he'd have to carefully dispose of her body— maybe put her corpse in that worthless mine that gambler Baird had sold him. Use some dynamite to cave a part of it in on top of her. He whipped the horse, which again made the bronc try to buck, but the animal did speed up some. The others were outdistancing him.

The first light of dawn came in a wide orange smile before the fiery circle rose over the distant peaks. Slocum walked back and forth trying to figure his next move. He had not slept all night, frustrated by Betty's abduction and the lack of signs or tracks; she had simply vanished. Apaches had taken her, more than likely; white men left footprints from boot heels. Although everyone had walked all over the area where she had been taken, trying to find signs and obscuring anything Slocum might have found.

Joe and Walt weren't to blame—no one was. Poor Meyers was beside himself over the loss. Slocum had to find Natise. What did he have to trade worth a white woman? He could recall the short, hawk-nosed chieftain—he would drive a hard bargain. The horses that Jones had would be the only things the Apache would even consider for her release.

"What you thinking?" Moses asked, squatted down, pouring himself a cup of coffee.

"I'm going to find Natise and you're going to find Jones. When you locate him, the two of you bring those horses to the renegades' camp."

"Where will that be?"

"Jones will find it."

"What if they kill you?" Moses looked into his cup of steaming coffee.

"Chance I'll have to take."

"I'm going too," Meyers injected, joining them.

"You better stay here and help Walt and Joe guard the crew."

"No. I'm going with you."

Slocum glanced over and read the determination in the man's face. He was dead serious and needed to be taken as such.

"You go with Moses and find Jones."

"No, I'm going with you."

"You don't know what we're up against."

"Makes no difference. She was taken when I was suppose to be guarding her. I'm going."

Slocum shrugged in defeat. He had no idea what good the little man would be going along, but there was no changing his mind. One brush with the Apaches would wipe out lots of that bravado. A wave of regret over having to be responsible for him soon subsided. They had to get Betty back and do it quick.

"You two mount up," Slocum announced, then walked over to the two ex-scouts. "You men keep an eye out on things here. We're going to try and get her back from Natise."

"Never figured they were that close," Joe said with a wry shake of his head. "But we're sorry."

"Could have happened with all of us here. The thing now is to get her back," he said.

"Be careful, that Natise is a tricky old bird," Walt said.

"I'll do that. He isn't going to be able to shake the Army for long."

"He ain't going to want to be caught with no white captive neither," Walt said.

"That's why we need to hurry. Keep your eyes peeled." Slocum indicated the camp of workers and the packers.

"We will. You be ready for anything," Joe said after him.

Slocum hurried to where Moses and Meyers waited. They had saddled his horse. He took the reins and everyone mounted up.

"Moses, we hit the flats, you ride south. Jones will make enough dust to see bringing those horses. Meyers and I will take up the squaws' tracks. They were headed east. Natise ain't going to be very far from the women and children for long."

"You two sure need to watch your backsides," the black man said quietly.

"We will," Slocum promised. "Just bring old Jones and those horses."

He sent his horse down the trail with the tight-lipped Meyers on his heels on the stout pony. Moses came after them. The hooves sliding and the sudden stiff stops of their horses going downhill only made him more impatient and anxious about her safety. Far below, the curtain of morning began to lift, letting the sunshine pour down on the greasewood flats.

How far away were the Apaches? He couldn't detect a sign of them. At last on the bottom, they parted with Moses, who gave them a salute and raced southward. Slocum and Meyers loped southeast to cut signs of the Apache women.

In a short while, Slocum had found the tracks and pointed them out to Meyers.

"They're headed around San Carlos. I figure they're planning on making a run for Mexico," he said, pushing his horse down the dry wash.

From the boot under his leg, he drew out his rifle and then tied a white rag to the barrel. Then he balanced the butt on his lap, letting the flag flutter, and led the way down the arroyo.

"That do any good?" Meyers asked.

"Depends what mood they are in."

"Mood?"

"If they were drunk last night, they might be mad as hell today. Then again, they might think it fun to talk with two crazy white men. You can't tell what they are thinking when you meet up with them."

"I hope they think we're funny," Meyers said, sounding grim.

"You and me both. Don't go for your gun when you see one. We've got to talk to them."

"I understand. You think they're watching us?"

"They could be." He was eyeing the ridges as they came into a place where the towering saguaro cactus studded the desert. To their left side, the steep slopes of Iron Mountain rose; to the right, the desert spread like a great brown ocean to a distant saw-edged range.

At mid-morning, Slocum saw the first Apache riding parallel to their course. He twisted in the saddle and shared a nod with Meyers. The rider showed no interest except in keeping his distance. Armed with a rifle, he wore a blue shirt and an unblocked hat.

Up on the bank of the wash, Slocum saw another buck north of them. Then two more joined in. They must be getting close to the main party.

"This what you expected?" Meyers asked under his breath.

"They act like they want to talk."

"Yeah."

"Whoa," Slocum said, spotting the figure of Natise sitting a big sorrel horse between two towering cactus. The chief cradled a Winchester in his arms, and aside from the black strip of war paint across his nose, he looked peaceful enough. Other Indians rode in to be beside him.

'Don't panic, no matter what," Slocum said to caution Meyers.

"I'll do my best. Your skin crawling?" Meyers asked, reining up beside him.

"Damn right. There must be twenty of them," Slocum said. "Boot that pony up here. We either win or lose."

"What do you want?" Natise demanded in Spanish with a cross look on his thin dark face.

"A white woman one of your men has taken."

Slocum was not prepared for the puzzled look on the Apache's face. Natise turned and shouted to a rider behind him, who drove his horse in close to converse with him, keeping a wary eye on the two white men. The two Apaches had a short parley, and Natise turned back ready to talk.

"We have no white woman."

"Is she dead?" Slocum's heart sunk with leaden dread. They were either too late or the little coal-eyed devil was lying.

Natise shook his head and shrugged. "My people know nothing about a white woman."

"No one took her from the camp on the mountain?" He tossed his thumb toward the mountaintop. Were they lying to him?

Natise dismissed the notion. "Too hard to go up there. We saw there were many guns and some white scouts were with them."

"You saw the scouts?"

Natise ignored his question and posed one of his own. "Why did you and the buffalo soldier ride through our women?"

"To divert the Apaches from the camp."

"Ha, we were away stealing horses from some stupid white men." Then Natise and the others spoke in Apache to each other and began to laugh. Obviously they had wondered about the senseless effort to scatter their women and children, and found great humor in the knowledge of the crazy white man's plan.

"I saw you before," Natise said in Spanish. "You once rode with Nan Tan Lupan as a scout."

"Yes. We met in Mexico." He recalled the man's surrender in the brushy canyon in the Sierra Madres and the return of his band to San Carlos.

"He has forsaken us for crooked agents who feed us tough beef and wormy flour."

"I don't work for him any longer." Slocum shook his head to show his disappointment. General Crook's departure from Arizona had left many of the chieftains thinking their only friend had abandoned them. They simply did not understand a government that removed chiefs from their adopted tribes.

"This woman is your squaw?"

"Yes," Slocum lied, figuring there was no way to make good sense with an Apache about another man's wife owning land and all that.

"They don't have her?" Meyers asked, no doubt unable to clearly translate all their conversation.

"He says they don't."

"Is he telling the truth?" Meyers asked behind his hand.

"Yes, I think he is." Slocum checked his stomping horse.

"Who did kidnap her?"

"I would say, the banker Moore must have her."

"If the Indians don't have her, how do we get out of here?" Meyers asked softly.

"Carefully, real carefully."

26

In the late afternoon, they rode up the canyon to the ranch. At last they were there—one stupid mistake after the other. Damn horses stolen—what else could happen? If Two Feathers hadn't captured her, they wouldn't have accomplished a damn thing. Ralph dropped from the saddle mumbling for Gates to bring Betty to the shack. He hitched his horse and started for the house, then heard the heated exchange between her and Gates. Exhausted beyond belief, he turned to see her fighting with the shorter man.

"Two Feathers, drag her ass inside," he said, out of patience with the entire operation. Gates couldn't even do one thing right.

Inside the cabin, he had her placed on a chair. Satisfied she would stay there, he rummaged through the men's things until he found a pint of whiskey and helped himself. The liquor burned going down, but before he had finished the bottle, it began to numb his pain. He stared across the room at her, trying to decide what he must do next with her.

Straight-backed, she sat up on the chair, like a dog ready to bite the first one close to her. He could see she was actually seething with rage. He began to laugh. They'd take that out of her. Yes, when the three of them got through with her, she'd sign the deed to Hell for them. Deliberately, he wiped the spittle from the corners of his mouth with his finger.

Gates was messing with the stove, building a fire and fixing some food. After they ate something, he'd start in on her. What did she look like without that dress on? It would be kind of interesting to see her naked.

"That deer meat's spoiled," Gates announced, coming in from the back way.

"You got anything else to eat?" What would go wrong next?

"Beans, they'll take a while." The man acted like the discovery of the rotten venison had left him without a brain.

"Cook them. Damn, I haven't had a meal in two days. And make some coffee—" He broke off, coughing his guts up again.

The sun had gone down. The frijoles were still boiling and hard as rocks when he tested them. He had tried to take a nap, but the hunger pangs in his stomach had cramped him so much he finally was forced to walk around the cabin. Maybe with some food in him, he'd feel better and be ready to take her on. She'd been sitting there the whole time like the damn queen or something—he'd show her.

"You aren't going to get away with this," she began. "I have written my lawyer in Philadelphia and if anything should happen to me—I told him in the letter you were the culprit."

"They won't find nothing when we get through with you," he said, dismissing her threat as nothing.

"You won't get away with my murder or taking the ranch."

"You'll sign the deed."

"No, I won't."

He stopped his pacing and looked at her in disgust. "Act

brave, lady. When this night is over you'll be glad to sign tha
paper.''

"Never.''

Two Feathers, who'd been squatted on his heels with hi
back to the wall, rose to his feet. He rushed outside and Ralp
followed on his heels, knowing full well anything that spooke
the Indian was his problem too.

"What's wrong?'' he asked, listening but hearing nothing

"Plenty riders coming.'' Two Feathers shook his head as i
he was disturbed by the knowledge.

"Gates, grab her and come on,'' Ralph shouted in the door
way. "We've got to ride out of here by the back way.''

"Where are we going?''

"To the Lady Luck Mine. There's a shack there where w
can keep her.''

He took her other arm as they hurried across the yard to th
still-saddled horse. She was protesting and trying to shake free

"Get your ass in that saddle or you'll be going belly
down,'' he ordered.

"You can't get away with this. My men will find you.''

"Crap on your men. Get to riding, and if you don't shut u
I'll gag you,'' he said as she finally swung up on the horse
He gave her reins to Gates, then went for his own.

When he had one foot in the stirrup, the half-broken bron
whirled, and only a quick catch of the horn saved Ralph fro
being thrown wide or dragged to his death. He managed t
painfully mount belly-down across the horn, and then barel
checked the horse before it plunged off into the catcla
thicket.

Trying to get his foot in the right stirrup, he felt the geldin
hump up, and in a minute it was bucking down the trail. Th
third jump threw him on the ground, and pain shot throug
his left shoulder when he landed on it. In disgust he rolle
over and started to get up. Several thorns and spines pi

cushioned his palms as he pushed himself to his feet.

He was busy trying to see them by starlight when Gates brought his loose horse back to him.

"Who's got her?" he demanded.

"Two Feathers. She ain't going nowhere. This horse shouldn't buck that much."

"Good! You get off and you ride the son of a bitch if you know so damn much about him and give me yours." He held his throbbing arm as he moved around to take Gates's mount.

"Sure, Boss, whatever you say."

The dim trail out the back way was steep and he looked back several times. He could see the lamps left on in the shack, but soon they disappeared. Going over the rim, he regretted not taking along his coat as the sharp wind caught him—but his shoulder hurt worse. Damn that woman anyhow.

"Will you tell the Army where we go?" Natise asked them.

"I don't ride for them any longer," Slocum said. He gripped the saddlehorn before him and stretched his tight back muscles, acting as unconcerned as he could under the circumstances. "Besides, they got scouts can track you, they don't need me."

One of the bucks on horseback shouted something threatening. As Slocum understood the words, they translated to something like "kill them and have it over with." There was a rapid exchange in Apache of many opinions.

In the end, the chief shook his head. The action set well with Slocum. His respiration rate slowed some.

"Go look for your woman," Natise finally said, dismissing them with a hand wave.

"Good luck in Mexico," Slocum offered; then turned and gave the stone-faced Meyers a nod to ride away.

The skin on the back of his neck itched as the two of them trotted their horses side by side down the dry bed of the wash.

Any minute expecting a hot bullet to crash into his back, Slo
cum looked straight ahead at the black ranges of the Super
stitions.

Then the war cries and yips cut the air. The fragile truce
was over, Slocum realized. He twisted to look back at the
oncoming horses, his hand on the butt of his handgun. Instead
the Apaches were riding off in the opposite direction, and in
relief he sagged in the saddle.

"It's over," he finally said to Meyers.

The man riding beside him did not speak for a long while.
Then he acknowledged with a nod that he had heard. The
trotted their horses about a quarter mile in silence.

"How did you ever find the words to speak back there?"
Meyers asked in a gust of breathlessness.

"Had to."

"I don't think I could have."

"You had me to do it."

"Tell me the truth. Were you as close as I was to pissin
in my pants?"

"I guess."

"Good. 'Cause I've got to stop or I will," Meyers said, an
reined up his pony. "Where is she at?" he asked, dismounte
and undoing his pants.

"Moore must have her. Jones knows where his ranch i
located. He's also got fresh horses and we need to meet hir
and Moses."

"They're coming to meet us, aren't they?" Meyers asked
finished and ready to remount.

"Yes, but we don't have time to waste."

"I know," Meyers agreed, and they galloped westwar
looking for signs of the other two men and horses.

If only he could change things. Betty's captivity was gnaw
ing at his conscience. They'd soon find Jones and Moses, an
mounted on fresh horses they could ride for this place

Moore's. She'd been gone for over a day and they still were assuming things. He rose in the stirrup, seeing nothing across the drab green greasewood. They couldn't be that far from Jones.

27

"How many men do you count are down there?" Slocum asked as he viewed the activity around the shack in the canyon. Several of the men were stirring in the first light. Some were busy at checking their horses' shoes, and others carried plates of food around. Smoke curled out of the rusty pipe in the roof. No sign so far of Betty, and that fact bothered him.

"Over a dozen down there," Moses said. "He has a helluva a big gang."

"Is that a star on that one?" Slocum pointed to a tall man wearing a black suit.

"Damn sure is. Why, that be the Sheriff Meeker from Florence." Moses shook his head in disbelief.

"What in hell is he doing here?"

"Looking for us?" Moses asked.

"I guess so. Dang, we almost rode into a trap. I wonder where the hell Moore and the woman are?" They carefully eased their way back from the perch on the rock to wait for Jones, who had gone to scout the south end of the main canyon.

"She isn't over there?" Meyers asked when they reached their mounts in the wash floor. As instructed, he had stayed

176

with their horses, and the disappointment on his face was obvious.

"No, she isn't!" Slocum kicked a pile of horse apples asun-
der. "The posse looking for us is over there, and no sign of
her or that banker." Had they gone wrong coming here? Her
life was on the line and they were fumbling around the coun-
tryside like bear cubs.

"What do we do next?" Meyers asked.

"Wait for Jones." He shook his head in defeat. Time was
burning a bigger hole in his conscience—if he hadn't been
jailed and all the rest, she might be safe.

"Where did Moore take her?" Meyers asked.

"I don't know. Mount up. We can't go north. The posse is
liable to ride out that direction going home. They acted like
they'd had enough riding around looking for us. We'll catch
up with Jones up there." He indicated the ridge above them
at the top of the canyon.

They were struggling halfway up the steep slope when they
saw the big Indian waving them on. Meyers had the lead, and
rode his horse like a man intending to get there first. Slocum
looked over their back trail and saw nothing.

"They ain't at the ranch," Slocum explained to Jones. "A
posse's down there."

"I figured something was wrong. There's fresh tracks coming out of there. Four riders rode out of there last night," Jones
explained as the others joined them.

"That posse must have scared them off," Slocum said
grimly. "Take the fresh tracks, Jones, it has to be them. It's
our only chance."

In a last look down the main canyon, Slocum couldn't see
the posse or the shack. No one appeared to be coming after
them. They needed to find Betty and soon. He drew a deep
breath of the creosote-scented air and rode after Moses as he
took up the rear.

In mid-afternoon, they drew up to the road to the Lady Luck Mine. Jones dismounted, and then with a nod of his head indicated that the riders had taken the dim wagon tracks up into the steep-sided canyon.

"My old mine's up there," Slocum said. "Wonder why they're going there. Must not be anyone operating it."

"Not much sign of traffic using this road," Moses said, leaning over in the saddle to examine the dim wagon rut that cut through the greening grass.

The familiar slopes made Slocum excited. There was only one way out of this canyon. If Moore had taken her up there, they were trapped and this might soon be over. Good, they were close. So she was unharmed—a grim thought of poor Milly swept through his thoughts. He booted the horse up beside Moses and rode behind Jones and Meyers. Perhaps she wasn't hurt—damn, he would thrash that banker with his bare fists if she'd even been touched by him or his bunch.

"What kind of business you doing after this?" Moses asked.

"Thinking Colorado might be a fertile place to light. What about you?"

"Never been there," Moses said. "Might be a right nice place to spend the summer anyhow. I don't like that snow."

"How much further?" Jones asked, twisting in the saddle.

"We better go on foot from here. The shack is just around the corner and so is the mine entrance," Slocum said, and reined up his horse.

"Here," Meyers said, and gave his reins to Jones. Without another word, the man set out at a run before Slocum could even shout for him to stop. Slocum drew out the Winchester and cussed under his breath, levering in a shell. "Moses, cover us."

"Wait!" Slocum shouted, running after Meyers. "Get some cover," he said, dodging to the side for some barrels. Bu

Meyers never acted as if he'd heard a word. He kept right on walking toward the shack.

The Colt in his fist, he watched the door open. A man in a sombrero appeared in the doorway, firing a repeater leveled directly at him. The dust from his bullets and the ricocheting whines sent Slocum diving for cover. He raised up in time to see the smoke from Meyers's Colt and the outlaw pitching forward face-down on the porch.

"Ernest, watch out!" Betty screamed from inside as a hatless figure rushed out of the door, blazing away at him. The whine of the bullets was loud. Moses' rifle cracked and the Indian stiffened, hit hard in the chest. He fired his last two shots in the dust before he crumpled in a pile.

"You're close enough!" Moore shouted, pushing her into the doorway. "You don't want her hurt, drop that gun and back off."

"I come to kill you," Meyers said, continuing his march. "Unhand her, you no good rascal."

The dumb son of a bitch wasn't stopping. Moore couldn't believe it. He reached past her, but before he could shoot, she knocked his aim aside and began to kick him. He struck her on the forehead with the gun barrel, and she fell down like a poled steer. Then he was standing exposed in the open doorway and that damn drummer was still coming.

"Get out here and fight like a man!" Meyers demanded.

"Go to hell!" Moore said, taking aim down the gun barrel. Too late, he saw the explosion of Meyers's gun barrel, and then a bullet struck his right shoulder and twisted him around. The sharp knife of pain made him drop his gun arm, but he raised it again and looked in time to see two more shots belch from the man's gun.

Next thing Moore knew, he was on the ground, blood spilling out of his shirt like a sieve. There was no way to stop it. Who was that little bastard—Moore's chest began to throb as if a knife was being plunged in and out. He could see the woman crawling away. He couldn't stop her. She took the runt in her arms. The dirty bitch and that runt had . . . finished him. Things were slipping fast, damn—getting dark, the sun was going down. Jesus, he hurt.

Slocum drew a deep breath, getting to his feet. It was over. Betty stood crying, hugging and kissing Meyers unashamedly.

"Did you see him? How brave a man he is?" She looked at the others for their approval.

"You did a tough thing," Jones said, throwing a leg over his saddlehorn and dismounting. He went forward and pumped Meyers's hand, then clapped his shoulder. "You did good."

"I ever need a real man, I'll be calling on you," Moses said, shaking Meyers's hand.

Slocum stepped in and shook Meyers's hand too. "You listened good. Point and shoot. Did you ever get scared?" He winked at Betty as she stood beside him.

"No more than I did with you and that Apache Natise." Meyers shrugged and took Betty by the hand. "Excuse us for a few moments," he said, and then he led her around the shack out of their sight.

"I'll be gawdamned." Jones began chuckling in disbelief.

"I ain't so sure it's healthy to laugh at him," Moses said with a wary shake of his head.

"It's time we made tracks," Slocum said to the black man. Then he turned to the Indian. "Jones, you will help them with the mine and ranch."

"Whatever they need."

"Good, tell them we had to run."

"I will."

The pair mounted their horses and rode out of the canyon in silence. At the opening, Slocum reined in. He had recalled a special invitation, and the notion of a certain Apache's dark brown eyes haunted him. A picture of her luscious body en cased in the deerskin made him shift uncomfortably in the saddle.

"Guess I could meet up with you in Colorado?" he asked.

"Sure thing." Moses shrugged, looking a little taken back by the news. "It's north of here, ain't it?"

"Yes, it's that way. See, there is a certain Apache woman kind of dared me to come back and see her."

"Slocum," Moses said with a wide grin, "I sure hope we cross paths again."

"We will, I'm sure. Ride safe, amigo."

Moses waved good-bye and rode off. Slocum reined his horse south and short-loped him. He crossed the Gila at sundown, forcing the horse to swim in the swift current. On the far bank, his mount shook a spray of water, and then he set out again.

There was a light on in the store's window. He could see it from where he sat his horse in the mesquite under the moonless sky and studied the dark form of the building. His pony stomped his foot, impatient to move, but Slocum made him remain as he tried to make his mind up. Finally he dismounted and led him to the corral.

The light went out inside, and he wondered for a second if he should mount up and ride on.

"It's cold out there. Do you wish to freeze?" she called out from the doorway.

"No. I've got to put up my horse."

"Don't be all night."

"I won't," he said, feeling warm already as he undid the cinch and jerked the rig clear of the horse's sweaty back. He tossed his saddle and pads on the top rail. Then he stripped the bridle off, shut the gap, and strode for the dark doorway. He could already feel the warmth of Mary Two Hearts.

Epilogue

After her divorce, Betty Wells and Ernest Meyers were married the following September. The Meyers family became prominent in territorial politics, and owned many successfu mining-ranching operations. Ernest served two governors or various mining commissions, and took part in many activitie to curtail stock rustling. The Meyerses built a Spanish mansior in a palm grove on North Central Avenue in Phoenix. It was razed in 1975 for a new apartment development. Some said i was a duplicate of the one on their ranch in the Superstitior Mountains, which had been destroyed by an earthquake i 1887.

Their children, Ezra, Liza, and Terrance, were all active i statehood activities. Ezra served as chairman of the Democratic Party for two years, and ran unsuccessfully in the pri mary for the first governorship.

Moses Teafeau operated a saloon in Leadville, Colorado He was shot to death in 1902 by a drunk in an alley whil attempting to break up a fistfight. No record exists of his mar riage or any children, though he reportedly lived with severa concubines.

Former U.S. Army scout Dirty Shirt Jones is buried in th

small military cemetery at Fort McDowell. He spent his later years catching mustangs and trading them in. No evidence of any marriage is available, nor are any descendents noted in the tribal records.

The breed Coy, alias Coy Brown, Coy Green, and other names lost in time, died in Tombstone from a rabid dog bite in 1885. His partner Lafferty reportedly fell victim to a mine cave-in near Wickenburg during 1891. Others say he was killed two years later by a Southern Pacific freight train while staggering down the tracks in a drunken stupor outside of Wilcox.

In September of 1880, Jim Crawford, the marshal of Goldfield, was gunned down by persons unknown at the edge of town while coming back from the funeral of a prostitute.

Pancho Villa, with his wagons and teams, went on to haul the municipal water from the Verde River to the hillside mining town of Jerome, Arizona, before he returned to his homeland. His activities in the Mexican Revolution are well documented, as is his demise, and have been reported in other texts.